HANS MAGNUS ENZENSBERGER

Mr Zed's Reflections
or
Breadcrumbs He Dropped,
Gathered Up by His Listeners

TRANSLATED BY WIELAND HOBAN

LONDON NEW YORK CALCUTTA

This publication was supported by a
grant from the Goethe Institut, India.

Seagull Books, 2021

Originally published as Hans Magnus Enzensberger,
Herrn Zetts Betrachtungen, oder Brosamen, die er fallen liess,
aufgelesen von seinen Zuhörern
© Suhrkamp Verlag Berlin, 2013

First published in English by Seagull Books, 2015
English translations © Wieland Hoban, 2015

ISBN 978 0 8574 2 821 9

British Library Cataloguing-in-Publication Data
A catalogue record for this book is available from the British Library

Typeset by Seagull Books, Calcutta, India
Printed and bound by WordsWorth India, New Delhi, India

Mr Zed's Reflections

THE
SEAGULL
LIBRARY OF
GERMAN
LITERATURE

In Place of a Preamble

One has to imagine Mr Zed as a person who keeps his ulterior motives to himself, bears his worries with composure and does not like to forego good things. Of a stout, round build, he will only catch the observer's attention through his calm and the fact that he is wasteful with his time. If he has a profession, he never mentions it.

His pike-grey eyes are wide awake, but anyone watching him will notice his short-sightedness. Along with his old-fashioned suit with its salt-and-pepper pattern, he wears a brown bowler hat that he usually places beside him on his bench.

When the weather allowed, one could find Mr Zed spending his afternoon in the park almost all year round. He kept away from the main paths, choosing a spot protected by hornbeams where, aside from a few hungry starlings, there was peace and quiet.

None of us could have explained how we first got into conversation with Mr Zed. By 'we' I refer here to a randomly assorted bunch of passers-by who occasionally stop and listen to him. Most of them went on their way after a while, shaking their heads. Others asked him questions or drew him into discussions.

At the end there were only three of us left. Why did we decide to share our conversations with a social environment that had never heard of Mr Zed? He himself, of course, is the true author of our collection, even though he never committed any of his words to paper as far as we know. Admittedly, we cannot guarantee the accuracy of our notes—first, because memory, as he impressed upon us more than once, is deceptive; and second, because we often argue.

Was it shyness or arrogance that dominated Mr Zed's appearances? Did he really say this or that thing? 'You're just imagining that,' said one of them. 'I know it very well,' replied the other, and the third suggested a deal: 'Let each of us be allowed to write what he wants. Mr Zed would have liked that.' And that is what our troika ultimately agreed on.

1 On the first or second day of our encounter—it was early April and the trees were preparing to end their long strike—Z. said that he wondered why we actually listened to him. He didn't feel old enough to have disciples, and he was the last person who would consider himself a master. We could not be confrères, he said, because he was not related by blood or marriage to the people who had come together here. Nor did he consider himself a teacher, for that might mean that he had nothing more to learn. Perhaps one could take him for an orator, but he lacked both practice and a platform. He needed no podium and was at pains to be brief. Whoever was looking for a leader had come to the wrong place, as had anyone who

wanted to gather followers around himself. We were all just passers-by who wanted to have a little friendly conversation.

2 'If you manage,' said Z., 'to find something that deserves your admiration, don't be sparing with this pleasant emotion.'

3 Z. said: 'Contradict me. Above all, contradict yourselves. One should always adhere only to what one doesn't say.'

4 One of us summoned the energy to reply. 'You're speaking in riddles, and I fear that this is your intention. I can't speak for the others here, of course, but, personally, I would prefer it if you expressed things less ambiguously.'

'You've seen through me. But do you think the ambiguity is just a whim? Please take into account that we have two hands. Left and right—they are easy to confuse, but certainly not the same thing. Our asymmetry has its advantages too. One needs two hands to wash oneself, change a baby's nappy or sew on a button. Our facial features do not mirror one another—if someone copied your passport photo and exchanged the two sides, you wouldn't recognize your face in the resulting collage. Or try this: first cover one eye, then the other. You will find that your perception is stereoscopic and that the world looks different depending on your perspective. The brain too, I am told, has two very different halves. So I conclude from all this that the striving for unambiguity is widespread but doomed to failure.'

5 While the questioner, an irritable young academic, was still thinking about how to parry Z.'s voltes, it suddenly started snowing in the late afternoon. No one was expecting that in April, except for a voluminous lady who had appeared in a mink coat. Freezing, the others brushed the flakes off their shoulders and ran for cover. Even the young scholar lost his desire to continue the discussion, and so Mr Z. was left sitting alone. Only the resolute lady was standing her ground. A silent man who had been there from the start also joined the two. He was wearing a well-fitting tailor-made suit and a pair of sunglasses that he never removed. There was only one thing that impaired his immaculate appearance—his mottled hair, which spilt over the nape of his neck as if he had neglected to seek out a hairdresser. Though

he seemed light on his feet, he supported himself using a walking stick with an ivory crutch.

The resolute lady watched the two men wordlessly. The snow danced before her eyes. All three waited patiently for the weather to clear up.

6 A few days later, Z. replied to the question of what he thought about death: 'As I can see that none of us are in the process of dying, it is premature to speak about it.'

7 'Supposedly, anyone who says A must also say B, and so on to the end of the alphabet. In my case,' said Z., 'I ask for this rule not to be applied.'

8 Concerning fame, Z. remarked: 'A famous person is only famous in their own bus. As soon as they leave it, they will find that no one has heard of them.'

9 Concerning art, Z. pointed out: 'No matter how urgently one advises young people against it—it will be in vain.'

10 'I hope, my friends, that you do not think me capable of any strategy,' Z. declared to us. 'I am not

your whisperer. One should beware of advisors. They are expensive, conceited and follow their own aims. Like the military officers in the general staff, they believe one can prepare oneself for any conceivable situation. I hope you do not think me capable of any such things. When it comes to me, you can rest assured that I keep my decisions to myself and leave yours to you.'

11 On the subject of tactics, however, Z. quoted a Chinese source from the fourth century BCE: 'If you are strong, feign inability. If you are full of energy, pretend to be lazy. Enrage your enemy and confuse him. Act weaker than you are, and feed his arrogance.'

12 On that late April afternoon, a burst of rain put an abrupt end to such deliberations. Whoever had an umbrella opened it and offered their neighbour a provisional refuge. In this way, some listeners who had only known one another by sight became more closely acquainted. No one thought of shielding Mr Z., who contented himself with putting on his old hat. He lit a cigarillo and saw no reason to vacate his bench.

13 Z. said: 'Getting by without the illusion of importance is healthy.'

14 There was nothing wrong with fortune-telling, Z. declared, even though no one had made such an objection. It was among the oldest professions in the world. 'The astrologers and their contemporary successors ensure variety, serve to entertain and are rarely more stupid than their clients. I like their boldness, and their forecasts are thought-provoking even when they are wrong.'

15 Z. impressed upon us: 'Reprimand me as soon as I threaten to become thorough.'

16 Asked for his opinion about atheists, Z. replied: 'What bothers me about them is their dogmatism. I also dislike the fact that they consider a higher intelligence than ours inconceivable. This assumption strikes me as more reckless than any belief in God.'

17 To the boisterous among us, Z. said: 'Whoever imagines that they belong to the winners will be put straight by their body sooner or later.'

18 When someone thought they could discern in him the first signs of the wisdom of old age, Z. said: 'That may be, but I am not falling for it.'

19 'Even threshing straw will turn up the odd grain. Nonetheless,' said Z., 'I can't recommend doing so.'

20 'Avoidance,' said Z., 'is a high art that is rarely taught and even more rarely mastered. Most people are hopelessly overtaxed by the mass of superfluous things.'

21 When he discovered someone resentful among us, he warned him: 'An envious person lacks imagination. They occupy their minds with what other people have and do, how they live and how they look. In so doing, they only harm themselves. They take selflessness too far.'

22 On one occasion, Z. brought along one of those robust Eastern European bags made of colourful plastic, from which he took out a pile of books. It was the first time he had lugged anything along.

'These are all holy texts,' he said, 'by which I mean works that never lacked readers, even before there were any bestseller lists. Why might that be? I have pondered this for a long time. Certainly, they offer the reader great variety. One is entertained with miracles and fantastic tales. Some passages are profound, others bloodthirsty. Literary criticism bounces off them. The solitary hotel guest finds them in the drawer of the bedside table. First prints are expensive at auctions and available for free at some stalls in the pedestrian zone.'

'What, do you want to read us something from these volumes? A Bible study meeting is the last thing we'd have expected from you.'

'We should not restrict ourselves to the Old and New Testaments. I can show you not only the fine reprint of Luther's translation from 1545—a definitive edition, highly recommended—but also the Babylonian Talmud, a Koran, the speeches of Buddha and even the Book of Mormon from 1830. Obviously the collection is far from complete—one could almost say that holy texts are ten a penny.

'What is notable is that each one of them believes it is the only one and has little time for the others. Most of them surprise the reader with peculiar regulations and prohibitions. One passage says that one must not let sorceresses live, a man should not have more than four wives, wine and pork must be avoided and a kid should under no circumstances be cooked in its mother's milk.

'Some of these texts refer to God as the actual author, while others allow that various writers were involved. Enlightened readers emphasize that one should not take such revelations literally and point to the complicated nature of the source material. It is not for nothing that their transmission through disciples, Hadiths, commentators and councils removed the apocryphal elements and sorted the wheat from the chaff. Strictly religious readers do not like to hear such explanations.'

23 A few older listeners complained that Z.'s remarks showed a certain lack of seriousness. It was not the first time they had had the feeling that he was lacking the necessary respect.

'I'm sorry you have that impression,' Z. replied. It was hard for him to refute it. Instead, he would make do with an anecdote:

'I have an Irish acquaintance who sadly cannot be here, as he travels a great deal—he works for a major airline as a purser. Before that he was a town vicar, even a prelate in the Catholic church in his home town, I think, until he had to give up his office under scandalous circumstances. The English language captures this in the elegant formulation that he was *unfrocked*.

'He asked me if I could believe that religions had had their revelations dictated to them word for word, right into their quills, by higher powers.'

' "Why shouldn't that be possible?" I replied. "Or do you consider it out of the question that there might be spirits in the universe who are superior to us?" '

'But that didn't satisfy him.

'This hypothesis, he claimed, would only make things worse. One would then have to conclude that the revelations you're referring to were a kind of divine jest, a practical joke, a prank played on humanity by these higher beings. As if they were revelling in our efforts to decipher and interpret the holy texts. That would at least explain their contradictions, and why their styles switch back and forth between dry lists, glorious poems, tedious war accounts, pedantic building instructions and gripping family dramas.

'But that struck me as frivolous, and I fell back on the teaching of Erasmus which states: All this does not bother pious readers, and if we do not intend to kill ourselves, we should spare them our jokes.'

24 The Epicureans did not doubt the existence of the gods but they held the belief that they were indifferent to the fate of humans. Z. objected: 'In the stories of the ancient Greeks, one always hears about the laughter of the gods. This assumes, at least, that humanity served to entertain them.'

25 'There's no such thing as the whole. Neither our science nor our imagination are capable of grasping it.' Z. often came back to this assertion.

Any talk of 'totality' made him feel ill. It was always motivated by some dishonest intention of a religious, political or intellectual nature. He, at any rate, was not only content with the partial—he cherished it and delighted in it.

26 When Z. began to speak of More and Less, we feared it would be an extended sermon—that is, More rather than Less. The threshold between excess and lack was unstable, he argued, the achievement of

equilibrium was the exception. Whether in nature or the economy made no difference in this context— there was oscillation everywhere. Longer or shorter waves, stronger or weaker amplitudes—that was the decisive aspect. Everyone could see for themselves how easily enthusiasm turns into boredom— for example, now, while listening. Determining the incisive moment with exactitude was not easy but worth the effort.

27 It was difficult to dissuade Z. from his inclination towards variety. For example, he praised the Chinese script, of which he had no understanding, for its 80,000 characters. He also praised the inventors of the Greek, Latin, Arabic and Cyrillic alphabets along with all their numbers and diacritical marks. This richness displeased engineers, he said, who prefer binary code with its sequence of zeros and ones. But he did not feel like occupying himself with texts that were only of interest to machines.

28 'Clubs are a fine thing,' said Z. 'They create a feeling of cosiness. That's why there are so many. Diligent sociologists recently counted them—there are supposedly 555,000 in Germany. The number of

members far exceeds the number of inhabitants.' He didn't know how many professional associations, parties, football and automobile clubs, firms, gun guilds, foundations and public bodies were open to him, but he had a high opinion of the volunteer fire brigade and telephone counsellors. One should be able not only to join such groups but to also to leave them without fear of any disadvantages.

29 When it gradually became warmer, Z. began to sweat. He removed his old grey jacket, and henceforth sat there in his shirtsleeves. But he did not give up his hat.

'Conversations about the weather are inevitable but inconsequential. One shouldn't let oneself be bullied by meteorology.'

The elegant man wearing sunglasses seemed to consider this advice superfluous, for he did not follow Z.'s example. He evidently refused to sit there in a shirt, no matter what the thermometer said.

30 Z. called the invention of the shaver a blessing. It saved the weary man who was tired of trimming his beard anew every day from the temptation of putting an end to this morning routine with the entic-

ing knife. He was thinking of Adalbert Stifter, who cut his throat one day because he was sick to death of the idylls he had invented.

31 Z. said: 'How often my teachers told me to concentrate! I preferred to distract myself, or—even if the metaphor is poorly chosen—to get bogged down in details.'

32 Z. commented dismissively on upbringing. It might be justified as self-defence against children but its disadvantage was that the adults thought they were more clever. That was a grave mistake, but one embraced by almost all parents, schoolteachers and professors. He comforted himself with a statement by the historian of science, Otto Neugebauer, who had supposedly said that there was no pedagogical system known to humans that was capable of ruining the spirits of all children.

33 One should read less, said Z. grumpily. It was a bad habit, and no less harmful to one's health than tobacco. 'If I had thought for myself instead of picking up books, or even newspapers,' he continued, 'I would probably have turned out brighter.'

34 Whenever a throng of Japanese tourists or a horde of wheezing athletes appeared and threatened to settle down next to us—which rarely happened, fortunately—Z. always paused and silently lit one of his stinking cigarillos, which aroused the intruders' disapproval. We only continued our conversations once we were undisturbed again.

35 There was too little appreciation, said Z., for the stupidity of poets, which bore remarkable fruit time and again. It remained a mystery, for example, what the young Rimbaud was trying to tell us when he declared: 'Il faut être absolument moderne.' He could only warn others of this demand. Nor did it gain anything from being pepped up with a prefix like 'post' or numbered the Second or Third or whatever. It always implied the laughable notion that one was a more intelligent, diligent sort—in short, simply more developed than the descendants to whom we owe fire, the bed, the shoe, astronomy and the gods.

36 The thing that matters most to oneself should be mentioned as if it were incidental.

37 Z. found it unfortunate that most people lacked ideas when they got worked up—this made their insults less effective. 'True mastery,' he continued, 'only reveals itself in invective. When Karl Marx called his opponent Bakunin a Muhammad without a Koran, this demonstrated not only his aversion but, most of all, his clear-sightedness.'

'He was surpassed in this only by that most gifted curmudgeon, Schopenhauer. And he was at his best when speaking about Fichte: "He said things that made me wish I could place a pistol to his chest, then say: You must now die without mercy. But, for your poor soul's sake, tell me whether you actually had anything in mind when you wrote that gibberish or were you simply making fools of us?"'

38 Z. advised us: 'If someone is out to provoke you, grind them down with complete calm. A self-important person will only be waiting for you to reject them. They want to gorge themselves on your objections.'

39 'Anyone who needs a guru has come to the wrong place,' said Z. 'If anyone is hanging on to my words, they should consider the fact that it's

nice at home too. Those who are asleep need no entertainment.'

40 Z. remarked that in the studios that were sprouting up everywhere, one could play the guitar, get sunburnt, lift very heavy weights, have one's nails and hair cut, make films or indulge in a Thai massage. But someone who wanted to study would be seen as a troublemaker there.

41 'Anyone who ponders over all the things they could do wrong is not to be envied. For the number of available mistakes is essentially unlimited, whereas one can count the correct options on one's fingers. According to probability, then, most things should go wrong. But, like participants in a lottery, we take our chances and cling to the illusion that Lady Fortune will smile on us. We are already happy to get a free ticket—instead of holding a dud, we think we've been given a new chance.'

42 'Whoever speaks of half-knowledge is guilty of boundless flattery,' said Z. 'A quarter would already be far too much, even for a polymath. For the formula $x/2^x$ very soon takes an infinitesimal value approaching zero. That comes closer to our actual knowledge.'

43 Z. wondered whether Montaigne was right when he wrote that one should 'leave politics to the more robust and less hesitant people who are willing to sacrifice their honour and conscience'.

44 Some of us had the impression that Z. was too sensitive. 'When some office forces me to pile up a rubbish heap of receipts and present it to them,' he fumed, 'I am seized by a physical disgust. I would much rather reach into a spittoon or a toilet bowl. It is not so much the insatiable greed with which the tax authorities pursue me that I am complaining about—what makes my gorge rise is rather that they constantly humiliate the tributary. The tax office is the bureaucratic nemesis that takes revenge on our joys.'

A few laughed at him and said he should follow the example of the Stoics whom he seemed to hold in such high regard.

45 Z. would not hear a word against Brehm's *Life of Animals*. 'Whatever objections scientists may have to it,' he said, 'I find swans exactly the way he describes them. He says that they are clever and wise but rarely abandon their peculiar shyness and restraint. And that their nature is characterized by self-confidence and a sense of their own dignity, as well as a certain imperiousness.'

In addition to their arrogance, old Brehm noted their reprehensible envy and a certain deviousness. That was as naive as it was correct, said Z. We could only deal with the animals by realizing how similar we were to them. The charge levelled at this amiable man of the nineteenth century, namely, anthropomorphism, was no more than a loanword.

46 Only solitary friendships were reliable, Z. claimed. An arch-enemy is worth more than a public chum. The man with the sunglasses, who normally refrained from comment, responded to this remark with a clear nod of the head.

47 When one of us complained about his antiquated use of language, Z. replied that a good dose of anachronism was healthy—anyone who entrusted themselves to the zeitgeist was beyond help.

Then he mumbled to himself: 'Unsurpassable. Studiously. Laudable. Quintessential.'

'Louder!' some called out. 'We can't understand a word.'

Z. raised his voice and continued: 'Plaintiveness. Confirmed bachelor. Foreknow. Besmirch. Effrontery. Coquet. When,' he asked, 'was the last time you heard these words?'

'No idea,' answered a young man in a bomber jacket. 'But don't worry about it. Just like clothes— think of the toga and the tricorn—words go out of fashion. And new ones are coined every day. *Tweeting* or *chilling*, for example. If you ask me, they're no worse than *coquet* or *foreknow*. I can understand why you miss *plaintiveness*. But that's no reason to get sentimental!'

'That,' Z. replied after a moment of horror, 'is something I shall take to heart. Nonetheless, I would like to say a word in praise of asynchrony. It is bad enough that we are damned to contemporaneity. A trend may relieve boredom, and currentness may deafen us with its shrill tones. It is all the more pleasant, however, to take a rest from the present. The music of Ockeghem or Gombert can help you to do so, as it is not old but ancient. Try it! Living at a remove from one's time is healthier, I believe.'

48 'What I like about philosophers,' said Z., 'is that there are so many of them. And that each contradicts the other. And that they do not shy away from speaking of things they know nothing about. To do justice to them, one has to savour what the great Hegel said about mediation: "It is nothing other than self-moving self-sameness, or it is reflection in itself, that aspect of the I which is-for-itself, pure negativity, or, reduced to its pure abstraction, *simple becoming*. The I, or becoming as such—this mediation is. precisely. because of its simplicity, becoming immediacy and the immediate itself."'

'No Dadaist,' concluded Z. from this quotation, 'could have put it better.'

49 When he noticed that a few of us were bored, Z. grew annoyed and said: 'Only boring people get bored.' Nobody wanted to expose themselves by protesting against this judgement.

50 It was not the first time that we were waiting in vain for Z. the following afternoon. Only half a dozen promenaders had convened in the usual place. It couldn't be due to the weather, for the sky was cloudless. The young man in the bomber jacket was

the first to complain. 'He's just letting us wait here,' he said.

'You're surprised?' asked the resolute lady in the mink coat. 'We shouldn't get annoyed over such coincidences—we should be grateful for them, as they provide some variety. Does it bother you that you came for nothing? I don't mind.'

'But he could let us know, or apologize.'

'I appreciate the lack of discipline here. After all, we meet where we do of our own free will. Anyone can come and go as they please. That's the difference between our little exercises and the kind of exercising one does at so-called workplaces. We could talk without Mr Z. Or are you worried that we won't be able to come up with anything if he doesn't appear? That'd be a bad sign. Any of us could take over his part. I'm sure that would be very much in his spirit.'

In this way, a different kind of conversation unfolded.

51 Z. was back the next day. 'It is impolite,' he said, 'to exhibit one's melancholy and burden one's fellow humans with one's worries. It is better to put on a brave face, at least in company.

'It also makes coexistence easier if one shows consideration for the idiosyncrasies of one's hosts. Among the English, as far as I know, it is considered inappropriate to mention something one is genuinely interested in—for example, one's work, lovesickness or the plans one is occupied with. The art of small talk, which strangers misinterpret as empty chit-chat, is a decoration for boredom. But appearing too witty does not go down well. When Oscar Wilde bandied *bon mots* about, he may have produced some immortal quotations but he made himself no friends. It's a different matter in a Parisian salon where *esprit* dominates as a neurotic compulsion.

'Even the unforgivable offences differ according to latitude and longitude. It makes an immense difference whether someone drops a brick, makes a faux pas or gaffe, puts their foot in their mouth or treads on someone's corns or tramples onto the piano or into the spinach. In Japan, a strict *No* is enough for someone to be considered impossible.'

52 'Only very spoilt people appreciate pictures that show as little as possible, or, best of all, nothing whatsoever. Rich collectors pay high prices for their *minimal art*. The excess of consumption corresponds

to a Puritanism in the living room—stark design or *Arte povera*. Poor people, by contrast, prefer to decorate their walls with lush bouquets, little pictures of saints and congratulatory postcards. I often feel inclined,' said Z., 'to do the same.'

53 When a sprightly pensioner demanded that he say something about money, Z. hesitated. Then said that everyone was always talking about it but nobody could quite say what it really was. Even a former president of the Bundesbank had supposedly admitted that he did not understand the mystery of creating money.

Nor could anyone say, moreover, how much of this phantom there actually was. For that, one would have to agree on the amount of money, and he, at any rate, could not find his bearings in that area. Apparently, one had to distinguish between M_0, M_1, M_2 and M_3, between black and white money, between the central bank's money, cheque money, fiat money and credit money. One also had to take into account the demand deposits and time deposits of banks and licensed deposit-taking institutions, with or without notice periods, pension claims, money market papers, monetary fund shares, certificates, TARGET credit and repurchase agreements. That, as economists never tired of assuring us, was a science in itself.

54 The question of whether one could touch it was also difficult to answer. Its state of matter changed from one moment to the next. It used to be solid, consisting of shells, cows or metal; then made of paper; then, anyone who was solvent thought it was a liquid. Victims of inflation thought it was no more than gaseous bubbles. Today, he continued, it mostly existed only in an entirely incorporeal, almost spiritualized form—as a series of electronic digits. The only certainty was that we all had to believe in it to a greater or lesser extent. So we depend on a fiction that makes Grimm's fairy tales pale in comparison. That was all he could say on the matter.

55 The energetic pensioner was not satisfied with this information. Z. had not addressed the difference between one's own money and that of other people— he would like to know more about that. That of other people, Z. replied, didn't bother him. Personally, he preferred cash. One could put it in one's pocket, it was dirty but discreet and one could see at once

whether it was enough for the moment. In addition, it was never a burden because it disappeared of its own accord. Money is like manure—it is only of use if one spreads it. Francis Bacon already knew that 400 years ago.

The questioner remained unconvinced, and went home.

56 Each of us was antisocial in our own way, claimed Z. 'One person is bothered by their neighbour's music, another doesn't feel like joining in with the crowd, a miser lets other people pay for them, whoever wants to stay sober is out of place at a booze-up, an unpunctual person makes his fellow humans wait and someone who can't stand losing marginalizes themselves as a spoilsport. And it is an affront if someone boasts of knowing nothing about football. In short, solidarity is not as strong as those who invoke it would have us believe.'

57 He wouldn't have a chance as a novelist, said Z. He not only lacked the patience and the talent but also his interest in marital crises, adulteries and divorces was quickly exhausted. He didn't even have an unhappy childhood to offer.

58 Z. said: 'Only those who least deserve trust vie for it. The business model of a bank is based on distrusting its customers. Savers, borrowers and investors should accordingly take the same approach. If such an institute promotes itself with the "green bond of sympathy" or "performance out of passion", it deserves to be swallowed up by its rivals. The purpose of money transactions, after all, is not to create a pleasant atmosphere or immerse oneself in states of arousal—the only goal of a bank is to make profits.'

Indeed, anyone who gave their trust to an institution only had themselves to blame, regardless of whether it was a corporation, a party or an authority. One could only grant it to individual people, especially when they didn't demand it. But anyone who could not summon such faith for fear of disappointment was to be pitied.

59 'Many who consider themselves enlightened,' said Z., 'attribute their conceit to archaic social forms, as if it were a characteristic of the aristocracy. Far from it! Snootiness never dies out. It doesn't depend on the social class with which one identifies.

'Every initiate looks down with contempt on all those who do not share their connoisseurship, whether they admire the wrong pop group, wear clothes that merit disapproval or lag behind the trend. This conceit is especially pronounced among dwellers of the Internet. They feel superior when they encounter others who are not up to date with the latest technology. They present them as people who have not yet digitalized their lives sufficiently and still live in the "carbon age". Presumably they think such backward behaviour does not befit one's station, even if an old-fashioned phrase like that wouldn't pass their lips.'

60 A bony man who probably belonged to a faculty, perhaps even the department of sociology, accused Z. of having a tendency to lecture people.

'I would hope not,' came the reply. He had always been cautious of educational institutions. He found universities especially tiring—there were always meetings going on there. And those who were at home there were tormented by reforms and paid badly. He, Z., was not only entirely unsuited to be an administrator but also a failure at understanding that desire for a title which had caused so many worthy women and men to needlessly ruin their lives.

61 The next man to speak up complained about Z.'s equanimity—it seemed as if nothing mattered to him. Z. conceded that he avoided getting worked up about every bit of nonsense. Anger, fury and outrage were precious resources that needed to be looked after. Fury passed quickly but consumed a great deal of energy. Quiet anger, too, could not be maintained indefinitely. Outrage, on the other hand, had a lasting effect—one should not squander it on insignificant matters.

It was entirely different with annoyance, which he reserved for everyday life. It was always in plentiful supply and dissipated quickly. The little outbursts it caused had their positive side, as they lightened the spirit. Anyone who disliked equanimity was neglecting the economy of emotions.

62 'How can I know in advance,' said Z., 'what I will think the day after tomorrow, when I can't even be sure what I thought the day before yesterday?'

63 A 'theory of everything', Z. argued, was impossible for theoretical reasons. As far as mathematics was

concerned, Gödel had said what needed to be said. That was why the standard model used by physicists was a mirage that withdrew from the researcher with each step he took. That did not rule out scientific progress. On the contrary! All evolution proceeded in this way. What was more astonishing was the widespread preference for seamless models and the longing for contradiction-free insights.

64 Could science be relied on, a curious philosophy student wanted to know. 'That is a question of perspective,' Z. replied. 'When you switch on the light, you are trusting the results obtained by a long series of researchers. You know—by name at least—Volta, Ampere, Ohm, Maxwell and so on!

'If you have higher aspirations because usability is not enough for you, and you ask what the truth is, then you should follow Hermann Weyl's declaration. For this German mathematician said: "I try to combine the true with the beautiful. But if I had to decide between them, I would choose beauty." It's up to you to find out what you prefer.'

65 'There is no free lunch.' What sounds like a narrow-minded sociopolitical slogan is, if one believes

Z., not to be dismissed. It was not only in economic matters, he said, that almost everything had a price. Everywhere—in daily life too, in biology, in technological progress, wherever one looked—one could find not only abundance but also abstinence.

66 'Nonetheless,' he added, 'an enormous, practically unlimited number of complex productions can follow from a limited number of elements and a small selection of formal rules. We find this in natural language through vocabulary and grammar, in chemistry through the formation of ever-larger molecules, in biology through the coding of DNA and RNA and so forth. A mathematician can develop the fractal beauty of ferns from a relatively simple formula—a few variables are enough to produce a large variety of forms. A walk through the woods offers sufficient proof of this. An anthill by the wayside is an even more impressive example. Or think of music's infinitely rich repertoire created by operating with finite rules of play. This manifoldness is a consolation that makes up for any renunciation.'

67 Z. had a predilection for obscure lists which he liked to recite unbidden. This time he treated us to a

botanical catalogue. He couldn't remember the correct scientific terms, he told us, the popular plant names were enough for him. He was delighted by their attempt to compete with the unparalleled diversity of evolution.

He wanted to know whether such names as pockwood, soursop, bittersweet or Swedish ivy meant anything to us. Awkward silence. Evidently there were no true plant-lovers among us.

'A pity,' said Z. 'So you know neither the hybrid witch hazel nor the common hart's tongue, let alone the bark-cloth tree or the garden lady's mantle.'

This gap in our knowledge could easily be filled, however, for he knew a place on this planet in which all these creatures could be observed comfortably in a single afternoon. It was the Botanical Garden.

68 That was a topic to which Z. kept returning. He hoped no one here had any objections to that luxury—he could show the way to anyone who appreciated the garden. No one needed guidebooks that wrapped everything in false glamour. They wanted people to believe that the so-called 'sights' consisted of castle ruins, palaces, cathedrals and other

antiquities. Readers were also pointed by forks and chef's hats to expensive restaurants which supposedly merited a diversion, or even a separate outing.

'I prefer a different location, one that such handbooks mention in a footnote, at most. I cannot imagine a more luxurious place to stay than the Botanical Garden. Here, you can choose between all the climates of the earth, from the tropical rainforest to the arctic tundra. Too hot, too damp, too dry, too humid or too frosty? You need only open a small door in the hothouses to find what you desire. In the open, you have the choice between ferns and creepers, tiny orchids and gigantic sequoias. The diversity of forms is numbing—no museum in the world has more to offer. And the whole thing creates the appearance of a discretion that quietly seduces instead of proudly exhibiting itself. The little plaques, with their old-fashioned writing, are all that reveal the erudition which is at home here.'

One could hardly imagine the effort it cost to plant this cosmos *en miniature*, to water, fertilize, contain and tend to it. What other people considered a nuisance seemed to come naturally to the gardeners, as if they too were glad to have escaped the noise of the outside world. In fact, there was generally a biblical silence in the Botanical Garden. It was never crowded. Certainly, it also served to inform people, perhaps it even had a pedagogical purpose, but it was, above all, a refuge in which the poor and the rich, believers and non-believers, cynics and the naifs could surrender equally to their imaginations.

'I have often wondered,' Z. closed, 'how such a utopian facility, which does not yield the slightest profit, can survive in a social-democratic, capital-intensive and thoroughly controlled civilization.'

69 Sometimes, said Z., he felt like defending superstition against a certain type of enlightener who made things too easy for himself. Such people were after absolute control through reason, but that was impossible. It was better, he said, to reckon with the imponderable. That was the only way to escape hubris.

Superstition provided the necessary means for this. One had to equip oneself with talismans and amulets, avoid ominous omens and persons, knock on wood and never say that one could never be struck by misfortune. Conversely, one should also wish other people a good journey, congratulate them on their birthdays and drink to a happy new year. He would like to see an enlightened person who was not familiar with such practices.

70 'Why is it,' Z. asked himself, 'that stupidity is invincible? Its genesis is a mystery to evolutionary biology. Its disastrous consequences are obvious, but why did selection not make sure that it died out if it causes so much harm? It can only be because it also improves chances of survival—there are many situations in which the ability to act stupid is useful. One can find a classic example of this in Jaroslav Hašek's brilliant novel *The Good Soldier Schweik*, which shows that the line between truly being brainless, boneheaded and half-witted on the one hand and carefully disguising one's cunning on the other is harder to draw than the smart alecs believe.'

71 Occasionally Z. sang the praises of routine—it was as boring as it was indispensable. The almost unbearable Kierkegaard even ascribed a religious meaning to repetition.

He didn't want to go that far. For there seemed to be one or two areas in which routine, like democracy, was out of place. Art, for example.

72 It was pitiful, Z. remarked, how the certified cultural exegetes were chasing after both the historical avant-gardists and the neo-avant-gardists—and the less there was to interpret, the more eagerly they chased. The yards of shelves full of commentaries on Malevich, Duchamp and the rest were growing as uncontrollably as the number of epigones sprouting up after them. The fact that the polemical energy of these 'works' had long been exhausted, that their producers had long since settled quietly and expensively into the global art market, had no bearing on this passionate striving. The commentators were evidently convinced that no amount of devotion was too much when it came to art. No philosophical, theological or cabbalistic argument remained unused in this marketplace. The less there was to see, the greater the burden of responsibility was for the exegetes.

73 'None of us,' said Z., 'can remember what is most important.'

74 'Really?' someone objected. 'As far as I know, the human brain has no reliably functioning delete button—neurological research has shown this. That

is why all attempts to censor the memory are bound to fail. Every law that attempted a *damnatio memoriae* has been futile. You know that terrorist from the fourth century BCE, who supposedly set a temple in Ephesus on fire in the hope of becoming famous? That Herostratus undoubtedly succeeded in this respect. Serial killers, tyrants and war criminals likewise live on vividly in the memory of mankind. Many of them even have memorials and mausoleums built in their honour.'

'You're quite right,' said Z. 'But aren't you confusing memory with recollection? The latter forgets the most important things if it suits it. But it makes its appearance when we are least expecting it, which is not always pleasant. Can we agree that our species remains denied the mercy of complete oblivion? In this respect, the monkeys are better off.'

We had the feeling that Z. had once again steered clear of the cliffs and beaten a careful retreat.

75 When he noticed that one of us had settled down in a folding chair made of transparent pink plastic, Z. launched into a tirade about the designer. 'Since the last successors of the Bauhaus passed away,' he began, 'these people have been busy making all

everyday objects useless. What they call creativity is actually a threat. Their triumphs include the abolition of the water tap, the construction of skewed shelves, the invention of lamps that don't look like lamps and provide as little light as possible, and seats that not only wobble but, like the famous chair by Gerrit Rietveld, also mock the human anatomy. The added value of these objects consists in being adorned with the names of their creators.'

By contrast, a man who had remained anonymous had, despite knowing nothing whatsoever about typography, succeeded in defacing the number plates of 58 million automobiles with the sausage-shaped letters he had designed.

One should, said Z., imagine hell as a place furnished entirely by designers.

76 Although there was no grumbling to be heard, said Z., it had not escaped his attention that some of us were scraping our feet. 'I can understand that. Perhaps I should not occupy myself with trivial stuff like water taps and electric razors. But I like to stick to the little things. A grain of sand can trigger an avalanche, and an itch can sour a sleepless person's

life.' Sometimes, Z. concluded from this observation, it was more important to have a handkerchief nearby than the Bible—in case of a nosebleed, for example.

77 One clear, warm Wednesday, the student who had often raised objections to Mr Z.'s words spoke out once again. 'Why is it that in all the things you talk about, there are no references whatsoever to things that occupy the public? Foreign policy, the economic crisis, large and small disasters, civil wars in Africa and the Middle East? You don't seem to care at all about any of that!'

'You're absolutely right,' Z. replied. 'So you're reproaching me for not addressing current events.'

'Exactly. I find that frivolous.'

'Yet you came back here. Even though you know that I ignore most of the headlines. That does not, of course, mean that I know better than the hard-working people who are capable of delivering an editorial or a commentary day after day.'

'But you act as if you weren't involved.'

'One doesn't have to be a Martian for that. "Shipwreck with spectators"—that's what the philosopher Blumenberg called this situation. I have the feeling that this describes our position quite precisely. What is more, we observe not only the case but also one another. You, for example, are not simply listening to me—you are also examining the way I observe others. And vice versa.'

78 The next time, Z. got worked up again. This time he was railing against anti-Americanism.

In the middle of our conversations, an ice-cream man had pedalled past on his tricycle, an old man wearing a youthful white cap with the Coca-Cola logo. A little sun roof adorned his cart, above which lots of colourful balloons bobbed in the wind.

'I have the impression,' said Z., 'that many of you are dissatisfied with the United States. Nuclear bombs, gun cult, Vietnam, Iraq, the CIA and so on and so forth. I can understand that. But, in the same context, this is usually followed by an attack on cultural imperialism. That makes no sense to me. For the same people who are offended by that are quite happy to enjoy the benefits we owe the Americans— they simply don't notice it, because the self-evident makes itself invisible. The old ice-cream man over there, for example, who looks as if he had stepped directly out of a Hollywood film.

'I would like to remind you of the many over-looked triumphs of American civilization—the crossword puzzle, the cocktail, the paper handker-chief, the pill, the toaster, the peanut, the zip, the electric torch . . . '

This catalogue, which threatened to become interminably long, was interrupted by a wailing that could be heard loud and clear in the distance. A crowd of children had surrounded the ice-cream cart and were screaming because their nursery-school teacher was refusing to buy them soft-ice-cream cones.

Z. watched these goings-on with a hint of impatience while the student laughed mockingly.

79 He had read somewhere, remarked Z., that the metaphor was the plague afflicting metaphysics. He wondered whether that might not also be the case in today's natural sciences. Theoretical physics and cosmology were especially susceptible. Since we had lost the grand narratives of mythology and religion, researchers had filled the gap with magnificent images. As Thales, Parmenides and Heraclitus had done in earlier times, they indulged, beyond their formulas, in an elemental poetry that dispensed with

experimental verifications. They had left the materialism of their fathers from the nineteenth century far behind.

Everything material had evaporated in their hands, as it were, disintegrated into quarks, quanta and fields. They effused over 10- to 11-dimensional strings, dark matter and dark energy, wormholes (!), quasi-particles and branes. Irresolvable questions did not intimidate them but stimulated their imaginations. Astrophysicists showed no inclination to agree with one another—whoever got a headache over the Big Bang could simply choose the Big Crunch, Big Freeze, Big Crumble or Big Bounce instead or content themselves with the Steady State. And if outer space became too small for cosmologists, they dreamt up a multiverse that multiplied until it was ash-grey. In future, Z. concluded, the poets would have difficulties competing with the poesis of the sciences.

80 In political conflicts, said Z., he was always struck by peculiar shared interests between the opposing parties: between the KGB and the CIA, the BKA and the RAF, or the Netanyahu government and Hamas. That had nothing to do with moral equivalence but was, rather, a matter of one side

needing the other. This mutual functional dependence resembled two slanted lead slabs supporting each other: if one were taken away, the other would come crashing down.

81 When he noticed that one of us was on the point of nodding off, Z. used it as an opportunity to speak about sleep. 'I am glad,' he said, 'that this is a mystery to science. The cause of this blessing from nature is, despite all expertise, unknown. Among the living creatures we know, there are short sleepers, long sleepers and hibernators. Yet no one can say why a mouse closes its eyes for 20 hours but a giraffe makes do with a tenth of that. The somnologists in their laboratories measure duration, depth and frequency, but there is a severe lack of explanations and no cure either for insomnia or hypersomnia. The one thing that is never in short supply is the dream interpreters.

'The only certainty is that humans cannot do anything bad as long as they are asleep. For that reason alone, one should not wake anyone unless the house is on fire.'

82 All people are theorists, said Z., even those who were unaware of it. The so-called man of action, for

example, usually claimed with a certain pride that he had little time for abstract ideas. He overlooked his own adherence to theories that are as old as the world itself.

Nonetheless, he argued, one should take the philistine's meaning seriously, for the relationship between theory and practice was more complicated than it seemed. Anyone who attempted to analyse every step while walking would never make any progress, as the necessary calculations were so intricate that even someone with a degree in engineering could barely manage them. It was similar with many other activities—for example, single combat, sexual intercourse or writing poetry. Before and after, theoretical reflection was not only helpful but also inevitable. During the act itself, however, it was an absolute hindrance.

83 Once Z. called out to us: 'A touch of *sprezzatura*, if you please!' not taking into consideration that such foreign terms mean little to most people. To calm them, he added: 'Not to worry. It is enough to know that even something strenuous should appear light-footed, not laborious in its execution.' Even the heaviest Newfoundlander surpassed us in elegance,

for it could distribute its weight between four paws. This showed that, like other things, the famous upright gait could not be had for free.

84 'Is it not true,' Z. asked us, 'that we cannot do without the word *not*, even though it is merely a particle that sneaks into our sentences? Even if it romps around in our grammar like a little kobold, we understand what is meant. Things only turn bad when the addition *hing* pops up like a growth, a metaphysical pimple with a domineering nature.

'But what does *nothing* mean? Since this question took over, theologians and philosophers have had a hard time with it. One could even say that they've only made matters worse through their ruminations and by elevating this remarkable word to a noun in its own right. Since then, THE NOTHING has haunted our language—a word of which I can only warn you.

'The first of the Greek philosophers implored us not to fall into its trap. Parmenides the Eleatic said that we should keep away from the nothing—not discuss it, not contemplate it, not speak of it. No one followed this advice, of course. Charles de Bouvelles, a mathematician, wrote a witty and crazy book about it entitled *Libellus de nihilo*. As so often, however, it was Hegel who took the biscuit when he remarked: "Pure being and pure nothing are, therefore, the same." Others have argued about the meaning of the following statement: One man says "Nothing exists" and another immediately hurls the response at him: "THE nothing exists." And the two are at loggerheads.'

85 Things were handled less conscientiously in what had once been called the 'hard sciences', he continued. An American physicist had recently attracted attention with a bestseller whose title already promised *A Universe from Nothing*. The quantum vacuum was simply not an unstable nothing from which many things issued—for example space, time, matter, energy and so on, to the last cufflink. Thus the author had disregarded the warnings of Parmenides once and for all. But that, concluded Z., either meant not a thing, or nothing, or even the nothing itself.

86 He failed to see what there was to celebrate about birthdays, said Z. If anything, one should congratulate the mother who had freed herself of a heavy burden on that date. One could safely dispense with bouquets. Most roses, like pigs, were only bred to be killed.

87 It was enough for him if he himself was observant, Z. remarked. But he was happy to take those present under his wing if they lacked that quality: 'And if you feel sleepy, and your eyes fall shut in the middle of the hosanna from the B Minor Mass? Only a monster could hold it against you.'

88 Who but merchants and economists could have dreamt up the idea that there was a balance between supply and demand? Everyone else, said Z., knew that the reserves of life and recognition would never be enough to meet our needs. And people were always asking about the so-called meaning, a further resource that was in very short supply.

In all of these cases, counterfeiters and conmen had to help out—from hedge-fund managers to gurus—for anything resembling a market to come about at all. Not even fear and the need for safety could be assuaged sufficiently to satisfy the consumers, even though insurances and the panic media did their utmost to stay on top of the demand.

89 Z. Asked us: 'How can something be less than zero? When negative numbers first appeared, they supposedly gave the theologians headaches, as they took them for the devil's deception. One can understand their reservations, for how is it that something which is less than nothing can constantly multiply? This seems to happen especially easily with debts. And why does x^0 equal 1? And what happens when one divides 1 by zero? Do you know why that's forbidden?'

Z. tried to shock us with such questions, but his attempts were in vain. We turned away, laughing.

90 Then Z. surprised us by unexpectedly spreading his arms and saying: 'God be with you! Godspeed! *Pfüat euch*, go with God!'

Some of us who understood the Bavarian phrase assumed he was saying goodbye to us, but he dropped his raised hands and said that those were all blessings. He wondered whether only believers were entitled to use such a gesture. Indeed, who had the right to bestow a blessing at all?

'Certainly it is first of all the priests, who are obliged to do so—from the pope, who famously includes the entire world, all the way down to the most humble deacon. But does the mealtime prayer not also contain the word *Benedicite*, and are we not familiar with the words of consolation spoken by the father to reconcile with his wilful children, namely, "You have my blessing"?

'Each case shows an expression of goodwill. The opposite of the blessing, the curse, is far less recommendable. It is much more strenuous, and saps the energy of all concerned, the strength of the one who places it as much as the peace of mind of the one cursed. There is no shortage of ways to undo the evil spell—for example, with a protective amulet or the invocation of a higher power, yet there is an ominous residue that they can never eradicate entirely.'

No magic could help the blessed to fend off the goodwill extended to them, however. Z. concluded from this that the simplest way to stymie one's opponents was with a blessing.

An old lady who rarely spoke out advised Z. in a quiet voice to beware of the dangers of arrogance.

91 The next time, Z. expressed the feeling that there could not be much to the music of the spheres. Even

the most powerful rockets could not change the delicious silence of outer space, as these zones lacked a medium capable of carrying sound. So one did not need to fear any noise pollution there. On Earth, on the other hand, we constantly had to cover our ears, for the air that sustained us did not care whether it transported a sonata by Haydn, a cry of pain or the frequencies of a pneumatic drill.

92 Fortunately there was a zoologist among us. He assured us that no living creature could hear everything. Worms and snails, he said, did not depend on the air to perceive what was the case— they did not need ears, vibrations were enough for them. Frogs were especially well off: deaf to all other sounds, they heard only the utterances of other frogs. While mice, whales and dolphins were considered experts in high frequencies, no other animal could match the bat— it could reach 200 kHz with ultrasound. By contrast, elephants ignored high frequencies and pigeons made do with 0.1 Hz, and were hardly bothered by their own cooing.

Z. praised the expert's elucidations and concluded from them that the speculations of cosmologists about the multiverse were redundant, because earthly ants, crustaceans and humans already inhabited entirely different worlds.

93 'Do you think,' said Z., 'I haven't noticed that one or two of you are taking notes? In former times, before there were photocopiers, that was supposedly common practice at universities. They had adopted this habit from the Greeks, who also took everything down studiously. They gave the words of their orators, hermits and philosophers the somewhat bombastic name *apophthegmata*. I beg your pardon for this expensive foreign word, if only because my Greek is not in the best state.

'"Silence is victory over every hardship that befalls you"—one of the Desert Fathers supposedly said. Not bad, albeit a performative contradiction.'

94 'So do what you must, not least in case you misunderstand me! Because one should always use a transcript cautiously. In any case, every reader will do what they please with the text in front of them. And they will not be the first, for publishers, editors, typesetters and printers already adapt, augment and manipulate a document, often without noticing it.

'For a hundred years, people read in *Leonce and Lena* how Valerio asked God for a "coming religion", until it occurred to a philologist to check Büchner's manuscript and he discovered that Büchner actually had a "commodious religion" in mind.'

95 'Textual criticism does well to pay attention to the smallest details,' Z. went on, 'because that is what it was invented for. These most careful of readers already argue over the tiniest errata. Unlike the writers who constantly make mistakes and whose manuscripts are often illegible. Hans Arp supposedly thanked his typesetter because the diligent man had accidentally corrected his poems.

'One sees from this that some errata and misunderstandings are to be welcomed. Anyone who fears them knows little about the temperamental nature of literature.'

96 For his part, he could offer a third interpretation of Büchner's comedy. How about a 'complete religion'? 'To be heard, a statement of faith needs not only a proper orthodoxy but also wild prophets, hermits and saints, zealots and reconcilers. Mystics who are viewed with suspicion by the high priests are

equally necessary. Most indispensable of all, how-ever, are the heretics—no church can do without them.'

97 'Gutenberg,' said Z., 'like the Chinese long before him, made type movable, yet created the immobile text precisely as a result thereof. The lead ensured a reliability of transmission tempered only by sloppiness and errata. Since the triumph of elec-tronics, this fidelity to the text has vanished entirely. Now anyone can do as they please with what they read. Democracy makes everything fluid. In this surge, it will soon be impossible to ascertain what someone originally wanted to say, or even write.'

98 Later, Z. said: 'Our encounters resemble the sit-uation at an aquarium. I don't know how it is that on some days there are only a few of us, while the next day an entire crowd appears. Is it pure coincidence, or are there some attractors that no one recognizes which ensure that agreements and conflicts develop within this small space? The people come along, hesitate, stop, say something or keep silent, and at some point they go on their way. . . . Don't you think that's wonderful?'

By this time all but two listeners had left. And so the meeting became an unplanned private conversation. The one, a bearded homeless man, was hard to understand because of his slurred speech. The other—it was the bony sociologist—took the opportunity to voice a suspicion. 'I have the feeling,' he declared, 'that not only you, Mr Z., but also all of us are under constant observation, not to say surveillance.'

'Whatever makes you think that?'

'There are rumours that suggest it. One of those here supposedly enquired more than once about your intentions and your personal circumstances.'

'So you suspect an informant. But who could that be? Please be more precise.'

'I noticed the quiet gentleman with the sunglasses, who always stays in the background and has never asked a question or expressed an opinion.'

'That's absurd,' Z. replied. 'The very harmlessness of our conversations makes such a thing unlikely. Anyone who came here looking for secrets would be an even bigger fool than every secret service in the world. Do you seriously believe that we are important enough to warrant such an effort?'

'So why are there people among us who take notes? I can testify to that.'

'It's flattering enough if someone makes the effort. I hope no one here will take this vanity as far as comparing themselves to Confucius or the Presocratics—whose work, incidentally, has only survived in dubious fragments. It is only a small step from your suspicion to a persecution complex. If I were you, I would let the rumours go. Paranoia is unhealthy. It can turn peaceful people into a mob, and I am sure that's not your intention.'

This gentle reprimand displeased the sociologist. When, on top of that, the brotherly alcoholic offered him his bottle of vermouth, he took to his heels and did not show himself again for some time.

99 'It sometimes happens,' said Z. at the usual time, 'that someone asks us quite unabashedly for our opinion in the street or on the telephone. They invoke our legally guaranteed freedom to express that opinion, but do so as if it were a duty rather than a right.' One would do well to turn one's back on such bandits. There were already too many opinions around in any case. Whoever uttered their own was

contributing to an unappetising pollution. If only for hygienic reasons, Z. changed his opinions more often than his shirt. As soon as they started to get black around the edges, he put them in the wash.

100 Arguments lasted longer than opinions, Z. claimed. They could at least be attacked and defended, which was entertaining and stimulated brain activity. The most deep-seated thing was usually what people held onto—their convictions. He did not advise divulging them. It was better to keep them to oneself as long as possible.

No one had expressed what he meant by all that better than Daniel Patrick Moynihan, an American senator, with the following maxim: 'Everybody is entitled to his own opinions but not to his own facts.'

101 'Imagine,' said Z., 'you are an ancient European hunter who kills a stag with his spear. What will he do with his prey? He carves it and shares it with his clan. He can use the hide as well. All that is left are the antlers. Perhaps buckles or buttons have already been invented—these can be carved out of the horns. But there is still some left over. The hunter grinds it to a powder. It tastes ghastly. Then he has the idea

of heating it up. That's more like it! The salt doesn't smell bad. His wife has prepared some flatbread dough. By chance a pinch of hartshorn salt lands in the dough, and it rises. At that moment, baking powder is invented.

'This means that, at some point, people try out everything that can possibly be tried out, no matter how bizarre. They will stop at nothing.'

102 A few thousand years later, as Z. saw it, Dr Samuel Hahnemann was dissatisfied with the prevailing medical doctrine. Perhaps, he thought, one should follow Paracelsus and heal *similia similibus*, like with like? It would depend on each attempt—trial and error would be the proof. 'It may sound improbable, but his students did not rest until they could provide cures from 1,400 starting mate-rials, including hydrogen cyanide, petrol, the bed-bug, the crayfish, mercury and the cross spider.'

One could, Z. closed, not deny one's respect to a species that came up with such things.

103 Regarding energy, Z. said that there was no lack of it—people simply used too much. This statement made us uneasy—we feared that Z. was planning an

extended litany on the subject. It began with the speculation that most transport problems would be solved by going everywhere on foot—the energy expenditure was modest. For his part, a breakfast of a croissant, an egg and a pear was enough to get going.

104 'Each one of you,' Z. continued his deliberations, 'knows the names of Messrs Watt, Benz and Otto. But what is a steam engine without a valve, or a car engine without brakes? Who will set up a memorial for those who ensured that horsepower— today we call it kilowatts—cannot do any great damage?' The reduction of pressure and velocity, he said, was a splendid task.

105 As if that were not enough, Z. turned to the hunger for energy in science. 'When Rutherford discovered the atomic nucleus in 1911, his experiment cost 70 pounds sterling. When Otto Hahn split the uranium atom a generation later, his apparatus could fit onto a laboratory table. For the first cyclotron tested by Lawrence and Livingston in Berkeley, a diameter of 10 inches was supposedly enough.'

The CERN facility in Geneva, on the other hand, covered over 600 hectares. The Large Hadron

Collider that went into operation there in 2008 had, it was said, cost around 4 billion euros so far and consumed 800 gigawatt hours annually. People hoped to increase its energy to 14,000,000,000,000 electron volts.

106 'There is no other economic growth that can compete with Big Science,' Z. concluded. It baffled him that our civilization covered the cost of such undertakings without wasting a thought on its returns. He observed that with satisfaction.

107 But not all secrets responded well to being aired, Z. warned us. Exaggerated curiosity was more likely to lead to disappointments than triumphs. 'Picasso supposedly said that he did not read English, and that, for him, a book in this language was a book with seven seals. Similarly, when he read something about Einstein's physics, it was all Greek to him. Yet he often understood something else, something that was of use to him.'

108 On one occasion, Z. spoke of Montesquieu's *Persian Letters*. A traveller from Isfahan came to Paris and found, to his surprise, that the king of

France, and the pope too, was a conjurer—the latter would have people believe that three were one and one was three, while the former insisted that paper was gold. Both were believed by many Europeans. 'That,' said Z., 'is only rarely the case today.'

109 'Most of us are social automata,' Z. declared. That was no miracle, and was hard to avoid. But there were exceptions—he knew a person who refused to use a computer keyboard. He avoided public transport because he was unable to deal with the machines one had to operate to pull out one's tickets. He was equally incapable of using a computer, and only knew the Internet from hearsay.

When someone brought up the difficulties resulting from this behaviour, Z. replied that activities of such kinds simply had to be taken care of by other people. He preferred to see to his own matters. Concerning his friend's confessions, Z. said he found it impressive for someone to be so removed from their time. But whether he should be taken as a model was an open question.

110 'I have noticed that everything is teeming with scenes—not only in Berlin but also in the provinces.

The art scene, the club scene, the film scene, the red-light scene, the hacker, collector, string theory and avant-garde scenes and so on. Many of these locations are overcrowded, as there are people who want to belong at all costs. I must admit that, in my case, they trigger an escape reflex.' Although he considered himself a friend of mankind, said Z., he would always remain a scenophobe.

111 The gaunt gentleman we called 'the sociologist' had reappeared, even though he had been offended by Z.'s implication that he was suffering from a persecution complex.

He wanted to know what one should think of Derrida's philosophical writings.

'You mustn't ask me that.' Z. defended himself with these words. One could just as easily ask him to form a well-founded opinion on the winners of the Eurovision Song Contest or the achievements of the German volleyball championships.

'Before you take offence at this reply, please be aware that I do not mean it as a snub to anyone. It should be seen as pure self-defence. For the number of celebrities has been increasing hyperbolically for some time—I am simply not up to the task of remembering their names. And so I protect myself with the magic hood of ignorance. I hope no one will hold it against me if I put it on.'

Our sociologist began a response, but because hardly any of those present had heard of Derrida, his protest fizzled out.

112 Manned space travel struck him as stupid, said Z. It was extremely strenuous, boring and scientifically unproductive. The absurd amount of effort only served the purpose of propaganda. The mere way the astronauts jumped about on their stations in their grotesquely inflated spacesuits was embarrassing to him, to say nothing of their bodily functions. Humans simply did not belong in the places these people would have to stagger to from their machines, like overtaxed beetles.

113 'No,' declared Z. when the conversation turned to the boundless greed of managers, 'it is definitely not a matter of how high their bank balance is. These people stopped needing money long ago— the only thing that concerns them is their status. They ponder which of the others is higher up the

payroll than they are. In the logic of redistribution, it would be pointless to tax them more heavily. Even if one could achieve that, which is unlikely, it would not produce more than a tip for the needy. Outrage over high and undeserved income is morally understandable, but it has no economic or social effects worth mentioning. Perhaps we should just leave them to their wealth, these idiots whose well-being depends on having the biggest yacht in the harbour.'

114 In some party committees, one says that some candidate or other does not smell as if they were from the right stable. Z. said that it was wrong to attribute this turn of phrase to agriculture, for any farmer would prefer the aroma of the committees to the fragrance of a dung heap.

115 The smallest words, Z. claimed, were the most important. One could do without such terms as 'triphenylphosphine' and 'plait classification' if need be, but not without 'I' or 'you'.

'These pronouns seem inconspicuous enough but they have plenty of pitfalls. Who, for example are *we*? What do you say?'

'At the moment, *we* means everyone with nothing better to do than listen to you,' said our indefatigable student.

'But it could also be all the inhabitants of this city or our small country, or the whole species.'

'That depends on whether you have the inclusive or the exclusive form of the first-person plural in mind.'

'It is not always easy to distinguish the two. Things become even less clear when the plural *they* appears. I recall a Polish book from the 1980s with the succinct title *Oni*, which is much the same as *they*. The author—I have forgotten her name, sadly—used it to refer to the Stalinist *nomenklatura*, whom she confronted. Her interviews showed up these former party grandees with notable success.'

'But what does that matter to us? We're not interested in these leftovers any more.'

'Fortunately. But please tell me who is being referred to in the following statements:

'*They* have now outlawed even 40-watt light bulbs.'

'On television, *they* said it would rain tomorrow.'

'*They* want to save the banks at all costs,' one man interjected, while another complained:

'On Saturday, *they* want to block Leopoldstrasse again.'

'If someone tried,' said Z., 'to replace the word *they* with the impersonal pronoun *one*, they would soon realize that this is impossible. At the same time, such statements assume that everyone knows who is meant, even though no actor is named.'

'Of course,' someone called out. 'It's always the powers that be. The capitalists. The politicians. The media. The bureaucracy.'

'Exactly. It certainly seems to be a nameless authority. A rather nebulous idea! Whoever speaks like that—and who doesn't?—is fluctuating between recalcitrance and *ressentiment*.

'Now I remember the name of that Polish reporter. She is called Teresa Toránska, and I raise my hat to her for this book. For she gives a precise description of the inevitable deformations of the people who belong to such an authority. And it doesn't matter here who *the powers that be* are or how they exercise their power.'

And with that, Z. did in fact raise his dented hat.

116 Another time, Z. wanted to know whether anyone present was on the left or the right.

Nobody was willing to answer the question.

'I'm glad to see that,' said Z., 'because this equally popular and outdated distinction only pleases people who prefer a simp.e political perspective. And they usually exempt themselves from this view. Otherwise they would discover that, without noticing, they were on the *left* and the *right* at the same time. The unadulterated progressive, like his conservative brother, is a phantom. Anyone who laid eyes on their own mental political map would find that it was as spotted as a patchwork rug. After all, even the avant-garde architect still appreciates his cosy old apartment with the Biedermeyer escritoire. And in private, the down-to-earth sausage manufacturer praises the innovations of molecular gastronomy.'

Our critical philosopher did not content himself with that. 'But why does your imaginary map make do with only two colours? You're forgetting the eccentric blotches, the white spots, the lacunae of ignorance. Worst of all, you're overlooking the grey tones of indifference!'

'You're quite right,' Z. conceded. 'Those are always the most expansive regions on the mental map.'

117 'One should put in a good word for alienation,' said Z. 'I am not the first to take such a stand. Suffering because of it strikes me as a luxury we cannot afford. Surely you too occasionally put your hands to your head when you expose yourselves to some communal experience. Watching any talk show is already enough. You will find that there are people who laugh on command in the studio. Or think of a pop concert, where everyone throws up their arms at the same moment, as if they lived in North Korea and had to celebrate the hundredth birthday of their dictator.

'The feeling of being out of place is not only inevitable in such cases but also welcome.'

118 A few who were prepared for an extended stay had brought their provisions from a *currywurst* stand. A young girl offered Z. a sandwich that he politely declined. She asked him if he was fussy.

'I cannot deny that,' Z. replied. 'But you should not confuse it with being pampered. It simply means that I trust my tongue, my nose and my stomach—the things nature gave all of us. Every cow knows which plants agree with it and which are better avoided. That is an inborn science one does not find in books. No one has to force down everything that society sets before us.

'You would be mistaken if you thought this only applied to food.'

119 One cannot be too sparing, said Z. unasked, with tributes. Instead of making them to those vulgar enough to lust for them, they should be reserved for a beloved person. There was no place for them in the public sphere. They were only really appropriate *in camera*, or, even better, *in pectore*.

120 Z. had noticed that he kept becoming an involuntary witness to people who enjoyed speaking about their dyadic relationships.

'I suspect,' he said, 'that this term comes from the vocabulary of electrical engineering. There, every contact can act to establish any given number of further contacts without impairing the current flow. I doubt that this also applies to erotic relationships. One already has to expect conflicts in a *ménage à trois*.'

He was simply unable to go beyond that and imagine a 32-person relationship.

121 One day, we were waiting in vain for Z. at the usual place.

'I fear he won't put up with us for much longer,' one man said; perhaps it was the zoologist who had enlightened us as to the abilities of bats and dolphins. 'And vice versa!' called out another, but he was quickly silenced.

When Z. finally appeared, he anticipated our criticism. 'Your reproachful gazes tell me all I need to know. You evidently want me to think for you.'

But he was too lazy, he said, to do what people expected of him.

122 After a while, an impatient man asked Z. whether the cat had got his tongue. How was he supposed to react to that without showing any weakness? Should he stay silent or acquiesce to a statement? In any case, the asker would have had reason to grumble.

Coincidence came to Z.'s aid. He pointed upwards to a silver-coloured zeppelin floating high above the trees. Everyone watched the airship become smaller and smaller until it disappeared, by which time they had forgotten the question.

123 Z. declared that he set no great store by his dreams. If he was not mistaken, the error of those who attempted to interpret them was that they were wide awake during their explanations. That was like trying to set down the outlines of a drifting cloud.

124 When it grew late one evening, Z. assured those who were still there that naturalness was a very precious thing. Whoever had lost it could only express themselves in an inhibited way. The much-maligned phenomenon of political correctness was only one of the many symptoms of the sad and self-pitying state of mind that afflicted many of our fellow humans. What was lost as a result had nothing to do with ideology, and could scarcely be regained.

125 Another time, a somewhat impertinent young lady in riding boots complained that Z. found fault with everything. Was he a troublemaker?

'That's a good question,' Z. replied. The tendency to complain about all manner of things was understandable. One could barely leave one's room without finding ample opportunity for it.

'The troublemaker, however, suffers from more than one weakness. First, he lacks self-confidence, meaning that he constantly feels aggrieved. Second, he lacks economy. Instead of spreading his resentment equally around the world so that the dose of poison causes less damage, he concentrates on what is closest and usually targets his neighbours, rivals and colleagues. But the worst thing is that he relies blindly on the help of some institution or other. As a result, he endlessly files charges, writes disciplinary and other complaints, petitions and warning letters, which he hole punches and files away in lever-arch files. It is he, of course, who suffers most because of his complaints.'

126 'In the marketplace of Marrakesh,' Z. recalled, 'there are storytellers who raise their voices until a sufficiently large crowd of passers-by has collected to find out how the story ends. As you can see, I have no plate for the small contributions which these narrators expect from their audience, nor the box which those lonely elderly people hold out who spread the good news on draughty street corners.

'However, you do not have to hope for or fear any attempts at conversion from me.'

There were enough criers in the wilderness anyway, he added. He was glad that none of us got carried away and made donations or expressed our appreciation.

127 An elderly man raised his finger. 'You don't want to tie yourself down,' he criticized. 'One often has the impression that you don't take any stance at all.'

'That,' said Z., 'may be because, unlike the beech tree in whose shade we have gathered, I am flexible.' He generally had no interest in pinning himself down. Self-descriptions were unreliable anyway. One had to leave the labelling to other people, regardless of whether the results turned out flattering or unfavourable. If, for example, someone said they were a devout Seventh Day Adventist, a rebel or even just an honest chap, this only fed the doubts of any sensible listener.

128 'It is said of some mortals,' reported Z., 'that they possess the odour of sanctity. Theologians, who

found a suitable Greek term for everything, speak of in such cases of *osmogenesia*. This notion seems to go back to the Egypt of the pharaohs but I know it persists to this day in some circles. Those who were around the saintly Padre Pio, who only died in 1968, could often experience this pleasant fragrance. It is said that it issued from his body, from the objects he touched and from his clothes. One friar who approached him was so beguiled by it that he almost lost consciousness.'

Z. saw that there were a few groaning sceptics among us. To calm them, he quoted Heinrich Heine. Many flowers smelt sweet, he had written in his *Travel Pictures*, even though they had issued from onions, meaning the bulbs. For the likes of us, it was sufficient if one did not 'smell foul down below'.

129 Z. said: 'Occasionally, one encounters people who feel the need to make a name for themselves. They must be afraid that one might mistake them for someone else. This is a matter of reflection—two mirrors in the bathroom could help solve their problem. To check how they look from the side, they only need to set up the mirror correctly. If necessary, they

should consult a surgeon, who would gladly help them get a more striking nose.'

130 'Society is a tyrant who needs no prisons,' said Z. 'If I could remember who said that, I would not keep his name from you. Does it ever happen to you that you have some brilliant statement floating through your head and you can never get rid of it?'

131 A thin 16-year-old wearing a T-shirt with 'syntech.com' written on it asked Z. if he still spoke on the telephone. 'Reluctantly,' came the reply. 'This device is a crass disturber of the peace.'—'But you still use it.'—'If there's no other way.'—'I don't understand,' said the inquirer. 'The telephone is inconvenient, outdated and unnecessary. People my age don't feel like wasting their time with small talk any more. A text message has 160 characters. Everyone's chatting, blogging and tweeting, and that's enough. You should cancel your phone service.'

Z. paused. 'You're right,' he said after a while. 'If I wanted to tell you about the telegraph poles along the country road, the up and down of the cables, about the sparrows that sat on them and the notes of music they wrote to the sky—you would barely understand me. But that doesn't matter. You just keep on tweeting!'

132 Theology wasn't quite what it had been in its heyday either. Z. said he regretted that. There had been a time when the best minds of Europe devoted themselves to this science. Duns Scotus, the *doctor subtilis*, or Thomas Aquinas, the *doctor angelicus*, would never have confused perfect with imperfect grace nor lumped together venial and mortal sins. One should consider, incidentally, that it was a scholastic, William of Ockham, who laid the foundation for modern logic.

133 'If someone guarantees you something,' Z. remarked, 'do not believe a word. Nothing of the kind is possible—you need only read the small print to see for yourselves. Be it an insurance policy or a pre-election promise, the message is always the same. Buy a basic electric drill and you'll be handed a brochure explaining, across 64 pages and in seven languages, that no one will be liable for the unforeseen. Depending on the culture in which one is located, there are various names for it: an act of nature, *force majeure*, or—why not go all the way—

an act of God. The Turkish phrase *mücbir sebep* apparently means a compelling reason. One is better off not knowing the excuses in Arabic, Urdu or Chinese. It is best to leave the party manifestos unread, dispense with the hailstone insurance and simply throw away your broken drill.'

134 'There are politicians in Europe who are aghast at the possibility of national bankruptcy,' said Z. 'To me, these people are like doctors who have never heard of the existence of tuberculosis and are surprised when their patients spit blood. Now, I am certainly no historian. But it is enough to read a paperback over the weekend—think of Carmen Reinhart and Kenneth Rogoff's heroic study with the excellent title *This Time is Different: Eight Centuries of Financial Folly*, published in 2009 and available for $19.95. It lists the national bankruptcies of 65 states. Among them, Greece stands out for being insolvent for half of the time between 1822, when it proclaimed its independence from the Ottoman Empire, and the present day.

'None of the politicians declaring their summit resolutions in Brussels and elsewhere seem to have heard about any of that. It is not entirely clear how such abysmal ignorance qualifies these people for top positions. One of the many particularities of their profession is that unlike doctors, pilots, roofers or drivers, they do not have to undergo a viva, an assessment, a journeyman's or master craftsman's examination or a driving test.'

135 'A 32-year-old Argentine from an upper-class home,' Z. related, 'was confronted one day with the question of how one produces toothpaste. Someone had pointed out to him that the Caribbean island where he was minister of industry lacked not only beans, milk and washing powder but also toothpaste. He would have liked to alleviate this shortage, at least. Yet he could not, with the best will in the world, see to such details. For he had also been made head of the national bank, and in that capacity he had to sign all freshly-printed peso notes.

'Although he suffered from asthma attacks all his life, he could not break the habit of smoking his beloved cigar, a comfort that was denied to most of his fellow citizens, as cigars were also in short supply. Perhaps this sad situation was a factor in his resignation from all his positions a few years later. Or was it because of his country's depressed economy?

'Shortly afterwards, Ernesto Guevara de la Serna, better known by his nickname "Che", became world famous. His portrait with the beret could be seen in most student haunts in the Western world, and many had the impression that he was, as Jean-Paul Sartre put it, "the most complete human being of our time". This suggests that cluelessness is not a prerogative of only our leadership.'

136 'What would you do if you came to power as a dictator?'—'Few people,' said Z., 'are less suited to this profession than myself, I think. But, very well, as you wish! First I would outlaw all motorcycles, as they are far too loud and far too dangerous. Then advertising would have its turn. It produces enormous amounts of rubbish, disfigures the landscape and robs people of time. But, naturally, I would be no more eager than you to live in a country where I was the dictator.'

137 The last speaker proved insistent. 'That may well be,' he began. 'But I still have the impression that you have an ambivalent attitude to democracy.'

'As you may have noticed, statements of faith are not my forte. But if you ask me so directly: Yes,

I have a strong preference for this form of government, perhaps because I lived under a dictatorship for a few years. It is only a shame that more was not left of it. We have long been overrun by abbreviations that do not appear in any constitution in the world—by the ESM, the EFSM, the IMF, the ECB, by a committee we did not vote for, and a euro group that meets in back rooms. Their only opponent—the so-called markets, which make them tremble in fear like a rabbit before a snake. I regret to say that we have entered a post-democratic condition which many seem to accept.'

'I don't,' protested the complainant. He declined the repugnant cigarillo which Z. offered him.

138 'The profession of the monarch,' said Z., 'has more in common with that of the marriage impostor than meets the eye. Bigamists and princes both find themselves involved in strenuous activities almost without doing anything. One cannot imagine how heavily the discipline demanded of them and the boredom they must endure weigh on them. Neither the admiration they receive nor the attention they enjoy can make up for the emotional strain they must undergo.'

139 One of us voiced the criticism that Z. seemed unwilling to leave out any topic. 'Isn't there anything in the world,' he asked, 'that you don't feel equipped to speak about?'

'I can only hope,' Z. replied, 'that none of you will mistake me for an authority. I am and always will be an amateur. I look around, have my thoughts about things, and am glad if someone teaches me better. Omniscience, which is a divine attribute, is something from which I am just as remote as you.'

140 Someone else took exception to Z.'s occasional references to the gods. 'Haven't you noticed,' he interjected, 'that God is dead? See *The Gay Science*, Section 125.'—'Who doesn't know that famous passage?' said Z. 'But are you sure that killing the gods is such a promising project? Consider that Jesus rose from the dead, and that Venus and Fortuna also visit us in all manner of metamorphoses and disguises. I conclude from this that the gods are in perfect health, quite independently of whether we believe in them or not.'

141 'There are always surveys being published about how much sex people have per week, whether

toothpaste should be green or pink, or whom one wants to vote out of office. But the pollsters have never asked people about gravity. That may be because no one knows exactly what it is. The gravitational waves Einstein spoke of have so far proved impossible to find, even with the aid of an interferometer which can measure tiny changes in the length of a laser beam with an accuracy of up to 10^{-19} metres. As I found out, that is a number with 18 zeros after the decimal point.

'People like us, who are more practically minded, are bothered by an entirely different aspect of gravity. We are annoyed when a glass of red wine falls over and ruins the carpet, when we wheeze our way up a steep hill on a bicycle, and when our knee joint hurts when we are invited to dinner and have to climb some steep stairs. A questionnaire would also reveal that, rather than stumbling, we would prefer to float like an albatross.'

142 A portly man who happened to pass by stopped, and called over the others' heads: 'And what's supposed to happen now?'—'With what?' asked Z.— 'With Europe, with China, with the crisis.'

Z., who had slept badly, yawned, put his hand in front of his mouth and said so quietly that no one could understand him: 'How should I know?'

143 'Durability is a funny thing,' Z. pointed out. 'The concern that things are gradually getting tight on our planet seems justified to me. There is no need to list the reasons. The demographers are raising the alarm, the climatologists are at loggerheads, the economy is slumping, it's becoming too warm for the polar bears, and so it goes on.'

Most people, he continued, were admittedly concerned with more immediate problems for the time being. They asked themselves how long the old tractor would still be running, noted that the roof was leaking in every storm, and that the new hip joint was not delivering as the doctor had promised.

Science proved that this was all connected to entropy. He himself preferred the famous Murphy's Law which states that everything which could go wrong will indeed go wrong sooner or later. That was a less complex interpretation, but one saturated with experience.

144 Z. reflected that as far as its durability was concerned, the elephant tortoise was far superior to us. 'To say nothing,' he said, 'of the advantage many trees have over us, as long as they are not assaulted by bark beetles and processionary or leaf-mining moths. I have been told that mammoth trees, lindens and cedars, last for over a thousand years. I doubt, however, that it would be a boon to experience the year 3000.'

145 Z. said: 'People who are occupied with the arts are insisting, in this respect too, on a special role. They agonize over the half-life of their products. They fear, often with good reason, that one can simply forget them. Like erosion, that is not a turbulent process but an inconspicuous one. The precautions some people take against it in their own lifetimes are very thorough. They resort to testamentary dispositions, estate planning, archives, retrospectives and complete editions. Posterity, however, does as it pleases, and usually turns out to be right.'

146 Once Z. wanted to know if anyone present was caused suffering by the flood of information.

Nobody raised their hand.

'Evidently this deluge can't be so bad.'

'It is,' a shy girl's voice spoke out. 'Too many TV channels. The Internet. My inbox beeps all the time. And every single thing gets stored!'

'I think', said Z., 'that I can reassure you. All of that will disappear again of its own accord. Not even the most famous traditions are safe from that. For example, the *Domesday Book* of 1086. Because the manuscript was so valuable, it was digitized 900 years later. Ten years on, the copy was illegible and the archive had to produce a new version. You see, hard- and software become outdated in a rapid cycle. Most systems are not backward compatible. The depots of the National Archives in Washington contain magnetic tapes from the 1960s that no one can decipher. Restoring them would require an unaffordable technical effort. So there is no need for you to worry— the flood of information will evaporate and trickle away entirely of its own accord.'

147 Z. had taken a break and was just about to eat an apple when a pretty young woman appeared, wearing green spectacles that were much too large, and took a tiny mobile phone out of her bag. Perhaps she was a journalist who had lost her way. She immediately fired a salvo of questions at Z.: 'Are you a Cancer or a Pisces? Do you have a business plan? Do you live alone?'

Z. stared at her uncomprehendingly. 'I'm not saying,' he said, and bit into his apple.

148 The reporter had noticed just in time that a hefty storm was brewing over the park. She put away her device and was gone. Z. was just about to start railing at the consciousness industry when he was interrupted by a thunderclap. 'There's the proof that there is a life this side of the media! We should stick to it,' Z. warned his listeners, but most of them had already been chased away by the sudden downpour. Z. watched them, quickly put on his jacket and reached for his hat. The silent gentleman with the black sunglasses had an umbrella with him, and helped the soaking Z. escape from the elements.

149 The next day, someone wanted to know if there could be such a thing as too much art. 'Absolutely,' Z. replied, 'especially art in architecture.'

150 'And what about the poets?' asked someone else. 'Are there too many of them as well?'

'As no one would suspect me of belonging to that profession,' came the reply, 'I can express my opinion *sine ira et studio*. Certainly there are many people with no ear for prosody, inflection or metre. And, as we know, poets outnumber their readers. In contrast to visual art, however, poetry costs little, hardly bothers anyone in the streetscape, and—aside from its rather environmentally unsound use of paper—it is generally harmless. Every one of you who feels the urge should therefore be at liberty to write poems.'

151 'However, those who cannot help themselves should at least have the courtesy only to write short books. Unfortunately, if one can trust the windows of bookshops, only very few succeed in this.'

152 After winning the civil war, said Z., the Sandinist government announced a series of poetry readings with the aim of improving the people's education. Before the venues were opened, hundreds of poets supposedly arrived, eager to tell off the *gringos* in verse. At the same time, however, there was a severe shortage of road workers and plumbers in Nicaragua, such that nothing could be done about

the deep potholes on the streets, and the water pipes
of Managua dried up.

153 Censorship, as one could read in Section 5 of
the constitution, did not even take place in the case
of revolutionaries, dictators or philosophers. 'Can
any of you,' asked Z., 'guess the author of the following lines?

> I heard the roaring, saw the flashing,
> Distant heavens drifted past,
> Emerged before they sank again,
> Sank before they rose yet higher.
> And when the inner struggle was resolved,
> I saw pain and joy unified in song.'

When no one responded, Z. said: 'All right then!
The author's name is Karl Marx. And while we are
at the merry game of guessing poets, to whom might
we attribute this elegy?

> But instead of bestowing on him glory
> The people of his land
> Brought the outcast
> Poison in a cup.
>
> They told him "Damn you!
> Drink! Drain it to the bottom

Your song is strange to us
Your truth we do not need.'"*

'The author, a novice at a seminary, is Iosif Vissarionovich Dzhugashvili. Better known as Stalin.

'I wish I could quote from the work of one great philosopher too, but unfortunately I have forgotten his love song. I can only remember the last line: ". . . and she knelt ecstatically in the moor."

'I daresay even a seasoned style critic would find it hard to identify the poet. It's Martin Heidegger.'

154 'Why don't you simply say "I don't like poetry"? That's forgivable. And your distaste has majority appeal.'

Z. was immediately conciliatory. 'I did not mean to offend the authors,' he said. 'Perhaps it's my fault that I often don't understand what they actually mean. But I will gladly name a Polish poet with whom that's not the case—her name is Szymborska.'

'Another Polish woman! Do you read all that in the original Polish?'

* Translated by Shubhra Nagalia, and published at www.revolutionarydemocracy.org/rdv9n1/stalpoems.htm (last accessed on 10 June 2015). [Trans.]

'No. As with other languages, I rely on the translators. We would be in dire straits without these badly paid labourers in the vineyards of literature, for there are supposedly 5,000 languages in the world. I appreciate this abundance, incidentally, even if it makes work.'

'And what's so special about your poetess?'

'Her words do not puff themselves up, yet each line is a surprise. One can understand every word, even in translation. So old fashioned, and so convincing! How did she do it? Unfortunately, she is no longer alive. She died as she lived—discreetly, but decisively. Hopefully the *sz* at the start of her name does not bother you. You can also dispense with the crossed-out *ł* in her first name if need be. Do you want to hear something of hers?'

155 'The first photo
   Who's the sweetie in the playsuit?
   That's little Adi, the Hitlers' son . . .
   The dummy, the nappies, the bib, the rattle.
   The lad, godless and unbidden, is healthy . . .
   There, there, no need to cry, that's better,
   Mr Photographer goes click
      under his black cloth.

Klinger's studio in Grabenstrasse, Braunau . . .
Solid companies, stuffy neighbours,
The smell of yeast dough, curd soap
    and so on . . .
The world history teacher loosens his collar
And leans over the exercise books, yawning.'

156 Nobel Prize or not, said Z., fame is a tricky business. 'How does Klopstock put it in his second ode to sailing on Lake Zurich?

Delightful sounds Fame's silver voice
To the pounding heart, and immortality
Is a great thought, well worth
The sweat of noble men.

Even if no one reads him any more, back in his day, when there were no talk shows, everybody knew what he was trying to say.'

157 Inconspicuousness, said Z., is a commodity that should not be disdained.

158 Whenever someone was described as being hard-working, Z. considered it a backhanded compliment. 'All that means,' he said, 'is that the poor fellow lacks a noble talent found in any cat— to roll up at will and purr with half-closed eyes.'

159 From time to time he read in the papers that some personality or other had recently lost all support, been expelled, excluded, dumped, booted out, thrown completely out of the game. Sent packing. And since then, in a word, things had gone quiet around him or her. He, Z., only showed understanding, perhaps even pity for such careerists when he heard that they were still alive somewhere up-country.

160 'Some of you say about me that I'm a sceptic. I wanted to know what that meant, so I looked it up. "One who examines, who looks around" said the dictionary.'

Z. had no complaints about such a description. It was never a bad idea to trust one's own eyes.

161 Z. had the bad habit of acting as if everyone could follow his allusions. 'You all know,' he said, 'that famous text from 1848 whose first statement reads: "A spectre is haunting Europe." I have the impression that the ghost of communism is still haunting us—in the form of an ectoplasm.

'Charles Richet, who was after all a Nobel laureate, coined this term. At his spiritistic sessions, he could ascertain that ectoplasm had a liquid, foggy consistency, that its smell resembled ozone and was somewhat unpleasant, that it issued from the moisture in the medium's mucous membranes and that it withdrew at the first disturbance of the séance.

'The notion underlying such experiments can be expressed in a simple statement: There's life in the old dog yet!'

162 It was probably inevitable that the conversation would one day turn to the critique of progress. 'A popular topic,' said Z., 'especially among all those who rejoice in progress. I can well understand their concern, for most of our triumphs have something devious about them. Nonetheless, I would propose a little game to those present. There is presumably no such thing as absolutely and invariably harmless products of the human spirit. If a person decides to, they can kill a fellow human with a harmless screwdriver. But what comes to mind when you reflect on the most favourable inventions of our species?'

This immediately triggered a confused chatter, until one person took the initiative and requested to conduct the search alphabetically. Several people led by example.

163 'All-purpose glue,' one could hear, and 'the ashtray'. 'The lift,' called out an elderly lady who was evidently happy to have one in her house. 'The bed!' These were followed by 'Button, bra, candle, chess, dictionary, fire engine, ice cream, kiss on the hand, lightning conductor, mayonnaise, meditation, onion, pasta, plaster, poetry . . .'

But here too, someone soon found a fly in the ointment: 'And what about the countless poems for war and agitation, the servile praise of rulers, the odes to Hitler and Stalin?'

'Good question,' said Z. 'So let's drop poetry. On with P!'

'Potato, pretzel, radiator, roof gutter, sparkler, spoon, stairs . . .'

The unusual noise caused a veritable barking competition among the dogs of some walkers, and a policeman who happened to be passing by stopped, surprised to hear: 'Toothbrush, tramway, tampon, taxi, umbrella, waffle, wastepaper basket, window, windscreen wiper . . .'

164 'I think that will do for now,' said Z. He only had a few small additions to make. Anyone with toothache would think gratefully of the invention of anaesthesia. And even the critical thinker would be reluctant to forego the flush toilet. And after all, anyone entering a restaurant should recall the French Revolution, which put the court cooks and messengers of the *ancien régime* out of work, forcing them to serve decent meals to ordinary people too.

165 'Isn't is almost a historical miracle that in some regions, for example, here, there is a lack of people who "are always forced to starve", as a song from the nineteenth century puts it? If anything it happens voluntarily, with consideration for health and the so-called BMI.'

'What's that supposed to mean?'

'The Body Mass Index was invented by a Belgian around the time of the Paris Commune, when the "Internationale" was also written. The World Health Organization elevated this measurement to a universal guideline. We were expected to kindly protect ourselves from obesity, diabetes and cellulitis, and return to the old Christian technique of fasting.'

In the light of Mr Z.'s considerable girth, his warning was received with chuckles.

166 On one occasion, he went so far as to say that whoever strove to be likeable at all times, to constantly behave in a 'caring' fashion, would do better to rely on their innate malice. Anyone who wanted to entertain a thought that was not self-evident had to go through the lonely school of misanthropy.

'You disappoint us,' someone interjected, 'because that's exactly what we expected of you.'

167 'Once,' said Z., 'it was popular to speak of the *lumpen proletariat*. Isn't it high time to examine the *lumpen bourgeoisie* for a change?'

168 'Did someone here call me an aphorist?' No one seemed willing to answer this trick question.

'What's that supposed to mean?' he exclaimed. 'That I provide you with calendar mottos instead of amusing myself, getting annoyed and arguing with you? I don't have to stand for this.'

The philosophy student, who had uttered the fatal word, said: 'Why so disgruntled? I didn't mean

to offend you.' Z. laughed and contented himself
with the apology.

169 Sometimes Z. quoted Lewis Carroll, to whom
he was rather partial: '"When *I* use a word,"
Humpty Dumpty said, rather scornfully, "it means
just what I choose it to mean—neither more nor less.
[. . .] The question is, [. . .] which is to be master."'

'Secretly, most people share this view,' claimed
Z. 'They simply don't admit it. Everyone thinks they
can decide what words mean. That usually leads, as
Carroll demonstrates, to unedifying confrontations—
especially, though not exclusively, among philosophers. Among married couples and politicians too,
there are often arguments simply over words. Such
quarrels can go on for years, but only serve vanity
and entertainment, not the acquisition of knowledge.
This can escalate to genuine trouble but should not
be confused with the strife that expresses itself not in
words but rather—much like grief—silently eats
away, and requires no partner.'

'Alice was unfazed by Humpty Dumpty's impertinent manner. She had neither strife nor grief
because of him, and always kept up her perfectly
polite and ingenuous demeanour in the face of the

adversity she encountered. Many people can't hold a candle to her in this respect.'

170 Another time, Z. got on to human rights. 'An uncomfortable topic,' he said. 'Anyone who takes it on risks looking like a blusterer, a spoilsport or a cynic. I believe it was in 1948 that the United Nations in Paris unanimously adopted and announced their declaration on the subject. Since then it has been automatically recognized by all members upon joining. At the moment, I think, 193 states belong to the organization. But there could be a few more every day.

' "Everyone," it states, "is entitled to all the rights and freedoms set forth in this Declaration." Its catalogue is like a bag of surprises. Everyone is entitled to the freedom and security of their person. Everyone can change their religion and convictions as they please. Everyone has a right to work, to just and satisfying payment, to rest and recreation, regular paid time off and a living standard that gives them and their families health and well-being, including food, housing and medical care. To avoid tiring you, I will leave it at this abridged version.

'The states that agreed to this declaration include North Korea, Iran, Somalia, Zimbabwe, the Congo and Sudan. I can't help but feel that the discrepancy between rhetoric and reality in this case makes a mockery of it all.'

171 'Naturally,' said Z., 'every nation needs fantastic tales from which it assembles its history. The destroyed temple, the virgin burnt at the stake, the Battle of Amselfeld, the partisan in the woods—the collective needs no novelist for that. Without regard for the facts, the nation invents whatever suits its purpose and believes in it. Archaeologists and historians attempt in vain to convince them otherwise.'

172 'How about,' proposed Z., 'sparing a thought for growth? A term from natural history and physiology, it seems. One can almost hear the grass growing at the word, or that majestic beech tree over there. Those growths know exactly when to stop. That's not the case with us. When the economy falters and the rates of increase fall, there is great wailing and gnashing of teeth. People claim that the stuttering machine needs to be cranked up immediately, as if one were dealing with an automobile from ancient times whose engine could only be started through the laborious use of a tool.

'Unlike politicians and managers, grasses and trees have an effortless mastery of exponential calculation. For according to this, with an annual increase of 5 per cent, they would have grown up into the sky fairly quickly. At this rate, a 10-metre beech tree would have attained a height of around 640 metres by the age of a hundred, had it not collapsed long before then. Perhaps learning from trees does not mean learning to win, but it might be enough to survive.'

173 'Small is beautiful. I fear this wise maxim is alien to the human psyche.'

An A-level student in the front row who was taller than all the others and often found fault with Z., sensed a personal problem in this remark. 'Don't worry,' he said, 'about being so small.'

Z. put his hand on the parting of his hair: 'Five foot four. Fortunately, ambition is not one of my vices, otherwise I would probably have behaved like many small men who suffer from delusions of grandeur. It matters little whether the context is a barbershop or world domination.

'I suspect that showing off is part of the basic genetic equipment of our species. Superlatives, market shares, growth rates, bidding wars over the biggest

diamonds, the biggest bonus or the best goal difference of all time. Even non-stop piano players fight
for a place in the Guinness Book of Records. The
bigger the bailouts and the more members states in
the European Union, the better. Of all the ways to
ruin oneself, that is still the most popular one.'

174 Sometimes Z. got onto the subject of school.
'Do you remember what they used to tell you about
the glacial valleys? Where the motorway bridge now
stands, the river supposedly once swept away leaf
huts, dead cows, uprooted trees, broken fridges and
gas masks. Only those who were lucky enough to be
standing on the escarpment were able to survive.
The teacher called that local history. Pretty chaotic,
the whole business. But that's out historical material,
our tradition. Whether we like it or not, we have to
be content with this chaos.'

175 'You don't have to believe what I tell you. But
perhaps you have some use for it. One has to take
other people's ideas, otherwise one's own will just go
round in circles.' Thus Z.'s justification for his tendency towards idea theft.

176 'You told us that you valued inconspicuousness, Mr Z.' said a man who had often stood out for his objections. 'But your language is standing in the way of this ideal, being—how shall I put it—rather high flown.'

'Anyone who thinks they can dispense with rhetoric is, as this venerable metaphor shows, on the wrong track. The ornamentation of one's words serves to counteract the audience's boredom and weariness.'

177 'Is that why you adorn your speeches with quotations?'—'Why do almost all people decorate their four walls with pictures, even if they are only posters or old photos? And animals do it just as much. Just think of the magpie, which steals everything that glitters and furnishes its nest with it.'

'Or bowerbirds,' the zoologist added in agreement. 'Their ornaments are extremely time consuming. They build huts and set up avenues which they decorate with hundreds of colourful shells, feathers, snail shells and Coke cans.'

178 'The whole exhibition,' the lanky schoolboy interjected, 'only has one purpose—courtship.'

'Precisely! The point is seduction. Just like a success-ful facade, or the tricks with which we attempt to give our words a little splendour. But do you really think it's only about sex? A reduction to graph paper and dice will satisfy neither our talents nor our senses.'

179 'The hatred shown by our architects and investors towards any kind of ornament strikes me as misanthropic. They invoke poor deaf Adolf Loos, and parrot the only statement of his that they think they know: The ornament is a crime. But that's a misunderstanding. This man had an imagination and valued elegance. They, on the other hand, skimp on any decoration because they are only thinking of their returns.'

180 We were expecting a new tirade against archi-tects, but were happy to listen to him because he always thought of a new variation on this theme. 'The house is conservative. Its purpose is comfort. And I'll give you three guesses who said that—it was the same Adolf Loos invoked by the misanthropic exponents of the building profession. These people should see an eye specialist, for they erect buildings that give the human gaze nothing to hold on to, and confuse an entrance with a mouse hole.'

It seemed logical to suppose that he himself had the misfortune of living in one of these piled-up containers, but we would have found it intrusive to ask Mr Z. for his address.

181 '*Que no haya novedad*! This is how people usually said goodbye in the Spain of old. It means: Hopefully there won't be any news.' Z. asked himself, and us, whether the Spanish always suspected the worst, or whether they simply wanted peace and quiet.

182 What bothered him about the usual talk of capitalism, Z. explained, was the singular. It was one of those portmanteau words that lacked clarity. 'Does anyone think that the conditions which are considered normal in Sweden and the Congo, in Greenland and Iran, can all be lumped together? The economic system being referred to can evidently live with almost every political regime: a military dictatorship, National Socialism, mafia rule, a communist unity party, apartheid, a Jewish or Islamic state, or with parliamentary democracy. What the singular sweeps under the carpet is the protean mutability of this economic form, which is the reason for its survival.'

183 'Among the culprits,' said Z., 'who are blamed for the eternal return of crises, the figure of the speculator plays an especially popular part. But the nature of this villain, where he comes from and what masks he wears—this might surprise some people. For in the language of the medieval mystics, "speculation" meant "an immersion in religious observation to the point of ecstasy". That's not only from Grimm's dictionary—it all comes from the Latin *specere*. *Speculari* means nothing other than "to envisage, to look around for something".'

'That's just sophistry,' the most impatient one of us objected. 'You can't call what happens at Wall Street ecstasy.'

'But you know there is more than one interface between theology and capital! Why are there *credi*tors and *debt*ors, why does the central bank speak of the *creation* of money, and what is the origin of credit? It all began in a more sacred context before being turned on its head through a semantic somersault.

'Luther was already suspicious of speculation because the Bible makes no mention of it. Soon all it meant to people was an idle, dubious rumination.

And finally it was the turn of merchants, who were on the point of taking risks and wanted to calculate their chances of success. In his dictionary of 1801, the staid Campe suggested Germanizing the speculator's name and henceforth calling him a "trading scout".'

'You're clinging to the history of words instead of addressing the matter at hand. You're making fun of us.'

'And you're laughing at me. But I still maintain that words tell us more than the politicians who bandy them about. How many people know that the bathroom mirror also comes from antiquity? A *speculum* only ever shows what is the case, and that is exactly what speculation does. It holds up the mirror to reality. No wonder its ratings are met with so little applause.'

184 'Holding up the mirror to reality—that's easily said. But what exactly is meant by *reality*?

'A Socratic question! This is how the famous old Athenian made his favourite partners sweat. He was certainly a wise man, but also a cunning trickster who had to be treated with caution. "Can you tell me why men are called 'men'?" How is poor Hermogenes to answer that?"—"No, I cannot, and I would not try even if I could, because I think you are the more likely to succeed."

'Naturally the old man did not let up but, rather, cornered him until his poor student could no longer defend himself. He could, of course, have answered: "Esteemed teacher, why do you feign ignorance? You know as well as I do what the word 'man' means in Greek. Everyone knows that. If we sought to define every word before uttering it, we would never get anywhere." But the young man was presumably too courteous to do that.

'Do you know what this reminds me of? A talk show. Socrates was probably the best-known talk-show host in Athens, and though his conversations created the impression of being private, word of them immediately spread in the decisive circles. But I must give him credit for one thing—unlike the other Sophists, Socrates did not demand 50 drachmas for each appearance.'

'One can say that in your favour too,' observed the A-level student, who didn't mince his words. 'Just like the Athenian trickster, you keep at us until we don't know whether we're coming or going.'

'Except that I don't pester you with definitions. Definitions are fruitless.'

With this, peace was restored.

185 'Theory becomes material violence as soon as it seizes the masses. That still applies today,' noted Z., 'though only to football.'

186 Not everyone took it at face value when Z. behaved in a compassionate manner. When, for example, he once emphasized how sorry he felt for the victorious athletes shown on television. Splattered all over with colourful patches, they were forced to commend natural gas, screws or milk chocolate to us. He did not begrudge them their earnings, but he did wonder what their achievements on the ski slope or the green lawn had to do with the insurance policies or beers with whose names they adorned themselves. Nor did he understand why they put up with the mandatory ritual baptism with the sticky sparkling wines that poured out over their jerseys.

'That doesn't dampen the enthusiasm of the fans,' said the boy with the baseball cap, who was irritated by Z.'s thinly veiled mockery.

'Of course not. But I'm not just thinking of the athletes. Why are they the only ones who have to suffer such impositions? Why do other people in top positions get away unscathed? I'm thinking in particular of our financial leaders. Aren't their tailor-made suits rather too colourless? Why might that be?'

'The manager caste,' one man suggested by way of explanation, 'doesn't depend on the fees of advertising agencies.'

'That's true. But what about our political staff? A party leader or minister is paid far less than any 30-year-old investment banker. Where, I ask, is the social justice in that? Do the party treasurers lack money? There's only one solution—politicians should follow the example of ski jumpers and racing drivers and entrust themselves to advertising.

'Enough of this drab and unimaginative dress! Bring on the patches and labels! How colourful the election campaign events, press conferences and parties would be! No interview without branded German products. That would boost not only domestic sales but also the proceeds from exports.'

'That's all we need. All at our expense! What about the interests of employees?'

'The representatives of wage-earners could also embellish their outfits with company logos. That would loosen up the pictures taken during tough wage talks, and with their advertising revenues, trade unionists could lower membership fees or fill the strike funds.

'In this way, each person would wear their own sponsor on their chest. It's always good to know who is paying. This would demonstrate to everyone what the old saying tells us and every sports programme teaches us: Honesty is the best policy!'

187 The flat rate was another one of those half-baked ideas that big companies make their money from, said Z. 'Why should it only apply to these tiny telephones you cling to? I would like to make the case for a little more courage. Why should we pay anew every time we take a taxi, drink a beer or go to the theatre? I, at any rate, find the bills on the plate and in the letterbox tiresome. All these endless account numbers and bank-transfer forms! Is that necessary? A flattened rate—is that what one would call it in German?—and water, electricity, rent, medicine and taxes would never demand attention again. Perhaps the bakers and dairy shops should join

in too, then there'd be bread and butter without coins or credit cards.'

188 'Have you noticed,' asked Z., 'that the advertising people have dispossessed the classics? Mozart and Molière, that was yesterday. Today the word *classic*—in English of course, for these people do not speak German—is emblazoned on bath-foam bottles, expensive pencils and cheese boxes.'

189 Then Z. laid into film music. It was intrusive, pathetic and generally superfluous. Every dialogue drowned in this murky slush. The sound engineers responsible for the mixing were evidently hard of hearing. The great masters of film often managed without any of this bothersome noise.

190 'Why,' asked one of us, 'are you in a bad mood, Mr Z.?'

'Is one obliged to *have* fun all the time? Then you might as well just use the word *fun*, if that's what you mean.'

'At your age, Mr Z., you should be tolerant and above such gybes.'

'You're right. I resolve to abandon this bad habit tomorrow morning, albeit not before ten o'clock, and meet you in good cheer. Until then, I bid you good evening.'

191 There was almost always someone prepared to defend Z. against his assailants. This time the philosophy student, who had so far been more visible for his attacks, asked: 'Which one of you knows what a curmudgeon is?'

The North German audience had no answer.

'The curmudgeon,' explained the budding philosopher, 'should not be confused with the caviller, the niggler or the whinger. For Mr Z. does not get worked up, he does not get loud in the manner of the bellyacher. The things he notices and laments scarcely surprise him. Unlike the sourpuss, he is not ruffled by the fact that humans are not all cut from the right cloth.'

This speech was silently accepted.

192 The following day, Z. was asked: 'Are you in better cheer today?'

He sneezed, blew his nose and said: 'No.'

193 At that, some of those who had lasted until then left us. But we didn't let it discourage us. 'What's the matter?' we asked. 'We've never known you to be so crotchety.'

'I was once in Lisbon,' Z. recounted. 'It was long ago. It must have been around noon. The streets were deserted.' He pointed to his wrist. 'I never wear a watch. In that sense, I'm a parasite. I looked around for a church steeple, one of those old-fashioned weather pillars that show the temperature and time along with the air pressure. But all the clocks in Lisbon had stopped. One had stopped at five o'clock, another at half past eight. No one had made the effort to wind them up. Today I feel just as I did then.'

194 'Sadness is a state we all know, except for doctors of the mind, who call it depression. A friend of mine who suffers from it recently started talking about the skin. It kept getting thinner, he said. The things people did to tighten it, smooth it and paint it!'

'Are you talking about me?' enquired the elastic lady in riding boots, whom one might have surmised to be somewhat familiar with such practices.

'Excuse me, madam! A little Botox, a bit of face lifting . . . if only that were all! No. My friend has much greater phenomena in mind. Most of what he sees, he says, seems to him like an ensemble of advertisements. Today's art, for example. It has embraced a supply-oriented aesthetic along the lines of "what you see is what you get". It doesn't get under our skin any more, contenting itself simply with the user interface. Some call that "content management". The thinner the screen, the better!'

The philosophy student felt compelled to answer. 'No wonder your friend is dejected. He evidently misses depth, inwardness. Cultural critics have always moaned that everything had become so ephemeral and superficial.' And to show how little he thought of such concerns, he added: 'Perhaps your friend is simply upset that his skin is ageing.'

'Maybe. But couldn't it be that he, in his sadness, has noticed something which has eluded you? One should not dismiss the insights of the dejected, even if one is in such good cheer as you, my dear chap.'

195 'And why do you dwell on such worn-out thoughts?' asked the A-level student, who, as always, was sitting in the front row. 'If you ask me, it's because you don't walk enough.'

Z. didn't need to be told twice, and left us.

196 He only returned one hour and half a litre of mineral water later, refreshed by his hike. And immediately began to recount what had gone through his head along the way.

'Obstinacy, lenience and melancholy—those are dear old habits. One stumbles on them rarely enough. But when one does, one picks oneself up, feels relieved and yields anew to the eternal up and down of which Montaigne speaks in his chapter on regret. All things, he writes, are constantly moving back and forth—the earth, the cliffs of the Caucasus, the Egyptian pyramids. Even constancy is nothing but a hesitant fluctuation.'

197 'Your placidity gets on my nerves as much as your pessimism,' interjected the listener whom we always just called 'the sociologist'. 'Decide on the one or the other! Personally, I see a contradiction there.'

'It is laudable that you wish to disturb my peace. But as far as the end of the world is concerned, something of which many a person has spoken too soon, that is outside my jurisdiction.'

198 'You would be better off asking yourself why we all have the time to linger in the park in the middle of the afternoon. Before, in the beer garden, it didn't seem to me that there were only tourists and pensioners sitting under the sunshades. And if you go into the city centre, you'll notice that business is booming for expensive bars and cheap snack bars alike. Who are these customers? Actors on their day off, tramps, truants, models, professional criminals taking a breather? I hardly think so. There is only one thing they have in common—none of them seems too concerned about increasing the gross national product.

'I mean no reproach by that—quite the opposite. Wage slavery is not one of my ideals. I am, on the other hand, always willing to take a stand for the art of dallying. Perhaps the full employment lusted after by economists is not so desirable at all?'

199 'Could I ask an indiscreet question? I'd like to know if there are any workers among us. A factory worker, for example.'

The philosophy student raised his hand. 'A few times,' he said, 'I worked in a cigarette factory during the term break because I needed the money.'

'A very sensible reason. No one else? Then it looks very much as if we are far removed from a dictatorship of the proletariat here. Not that the working class is invisible—any passer-by can observe it most clearly on building sites, if only because of the countless signs and barriers, as well as the noise they produce. Occasionally, the workers become conspicuous through their strikes as well as the police whistles the trade unions supply them with.

'Apart from that? No comparison at all to earlier times. Production seems to occur mostly in secret. This is probably due to the career of so-called services. The group of people who manufacture something is far smaller than the enormous number of shop assistants, sales representatives, office workers and drivers—as with farmers, who have likewise shrunk to a minority. Supposedly, only two per cent of working people are still employed in agriculture. If I am not mistaken, that is less than the many who busy themselves with financial transactions, advertising or the wearing-out of media products.'

'You find that peculiar?'

'It requires explaining, yes. Admittedly, most of us no longer notice the extreme improbability of such a condition. But as soon as one starts thinking about it, it seems extremely unstable—like the activity of an artiste demonstrating a hair-raising balancing act. And we who are chatting here in the park constitute, for a few hours at least, the hard boiled audience at the event.'

No one interrupted Z. to rebut him, least of all the two old ladies on the bench whose knitting needles glittered in the sun.

200 A young couple wanted to know why Z. was avoiding a topic which most people never tired of discussing. 'No doubt you mean the conversations one can involuntarily witness in train compartments and waiting rooms. They usually revolve around dietary requirements, gynaecology, pets and trouble with the plumber when the tap is dripping.'

'No. We would like you to share your views on sexuality.'

'That,' said Z., 'is something I cannot bring myself to do, for I know as little about it as you do. You'd be better off consulting an agony aunt or one of the numerous Internet forums. But if you insist . . .'

'Yes,' they both said.

'Well, then I would like to praise the imagination of the creator, or alternatively evolution, for the idea of inventing several sexes at once has been a source of incredible stimulations and commotions. There must be more behind this than the necessity of procreation. If things had gone no further than the simple procedures of viruses and amoebas—splitting once, full stop—then there would be no families, no marriages, no dangerous liaisons and no singles. The registry offices, divorce lawyers and relationship therapists would be out of work. That would still be bearable, but things would look grim for literature, film and television without Adam and Eve, Tristan and Isolde, Romeo and Juliet and so on. Even if this trick of nature can lead to unpleasant complications, who would want to be without it?'

Some people wondered whether this brief response was much help to the young couple.

201 'You hesitate?' asked Z. 'Surely you don't think I'm trying to discourage you? Far from it. We all know that resignation does not exist in nature— we should avoid it too. Naturally, there will be no lack of people standing in the way of your happiness,

who will do more than advise against it. Some will trip you up, step on your toes, come down on you. It can't be a coincidence that there are so many ways to put it. It's best to trust that the saboteurs of your affection will start by shooting themselves in the foot and then, after digging their own graves, commit slow suicide. For this hope too, as you can see, there is no shortage of suitable expressions.'

202 'Particular care is advised when persons in uniform are looking after you. I say that to anyone who fears for their safety. Beware of bodyguards, and keep away from so-called law enforcement! You should know that these people are not there to guard *your* body, and that they are never remotely interested in *your* security. How does one tell the overseers apart from the hooligans and hell-raisers? That's difficult not only in Syria, Iran or Russia but also in your immediate vicinity.'

203 'How hard it is to be lonely!' Z. did not leave it at this deep insight. 'That, my friends, is known not only to the German pop song—the business world knows it too. Whoever needs allies should turn to the German Associations Forum in Bonn. It

offers over 14,000 addresses for anyone who does not want to work away in isolation but lend weight and political influence to their cause. That obviously requires managers and personal offices. There is no lack of the corresponding staff. If need be, one can also seek out the German Society for Association Management which is, also, based in Bonn.

'So this is a veritable treasure trove! As no one can remember what's available there, I've brought along a note. Can I read out some of it?

'We have the Inspection Collective for Masons, the Association of Professional Wrestlers, the Association of Environmental Remediators . . . shall I stop?'

'No!'

'So we continue with the General Association of Dog Lovers (GADL), Aeternitas Consumer Initiative for Undertaker Culture and the Soft Foam Industry Association! Sadly, the list offers no results for anyone seeking representatives of nuclear reactors. I also miss the Association of Sewing Machine Needle Manufacturers, which someone mentioned to me the other day. But perhaps this search for a needle in a haystack was simply beyond my abilities.'

'And what do you conclude from your research?'

'We shouldn't worry about the representation of our interests, however bizarre or obscure they might be. Some executive or other will look after them.'

204 The art of remaining silent in public, Z. lamented, was increasingly being brought into discredit. Most people were not content with a bit of lip—they constantly had to shoot their mouths off. The number of people who had mastered the art of restraint was growing smaller all the time.

'An art you don't know anything about,' shouted an impertinent 12-year-old wearing a purple baseball cap. He was one of those pupils from the nearby secondary school who sometimes got together in the park after school finished to smoke a joint in secret. A sullen silence was Z.'s only response to this interjection, which had made sense to us.

205 Soon afterwards, it occurred to him to warn us of excessive education. It was just as addictive as smoking. Whoever indulged in it for long enough could only escape the addiction with difficulty. The danger of overdosing was always at hand, even if the victim had long grown tired of the drug.

'Believe me, I know what I'm talking about! Should I, at my advanced age, sit down in the back row as a guest student, take a Chinese course and work through all sorts of tests and examinations? Lifelong learning—how can one fend off this imposition? What would you advise?'

'In your case,' replied a stranger whom we had never noticed before, 'it's too late to change anything. Education is like innocence—there's no way back to a blank slate. You'll never make it as a noble savage. You should learn to deal with that.'

206 'Peculiar that none of you have mentioned marriage. Monogamy,' said Z., 'is a remarkable invention that, after all, defies all probability—far more interesting and puzzling than adultery which has already been dealt with in far too many books.'

207 'As you know, there are writers who copy themselves without noticing. Others draw on established methods to avoid this danger. One of these is the pseudonym—it offers the author not only a certain protection but also a new identity. Reproached for not using his real name, Casanova is reported to have said: "The alphabet belongs to me."'

208 When one of us brought up the question of copyright, Z. shrugged his shoulders and said that, personally, he did not have any difficulties with it. 'As you may have noticed, we make do without tickets here. It is also pleasant that one can still ask for a glass of water or a light without showing one's credit card. What troubles me, however, is the shabbiness of the so-called "net dwellers". They have long internalized the same narrow-mindedness of which they accuse their elders. Without noticing, they rub their hands while hunting bargains, appear wherever there's something to be had for free and are smugly convinced that tight is right.'

209 The other day, he—Z.—had chanced upon an eighteenth-century correspondence in which the author addressed the subject of intellectual property. 'I never trust accusations of plagiarism,' he had written, 'in fact, I despise the people who make such claims, and despise yet more their agents, the petty fools who repeat such things. A rich man should not complain that he has been robbed of a few paltry coins.' Puff was part of the trade, Z. closed, and so was stealing.

210 Z. drew a ∞ in the air and said: 'No doubt you are familiar with this pretty symbol. Not only philosophers, theologians and mathematicians are irresistibly attracted to infinity—quick-witted children also exercise their imaginations with the idea that there is supposedly something which never stops. Why is it that one finds it easier to warm to the infinite than to finitude? Because very few people welcome the fact that they are mortal.'

211 Adolescence, Z. declared, was unenviable. 'I'm not referring at all to the "youth of today". Statements that begin with those words do not merit being taken seriously. Often enough, comparisons with older generations do not turn out favourably for the latter.

'One should therefore cleave more to those developments unconnected to specific generations. Everyone who has got the metamorphosis in question over and done with knows that it is fairly strenuous. Progressing from the pupa to the imago is no mean feat. Just think what beetles and butterflies have to endure—the physical reconstruction, the shedding of skin and the hormonal storms!'

212 'Fortunately, one soon forgets this painful phase. Anyone who wanted to remember everything that happened to them would require psychiatric treatment.'

213 'In my praise of forgetfulness, I forgot that one cannot rely on it. Do you find that too? You think some incident or other is completely in the past—whether no more than an insult or embarrassment, or rather a severe trauma. And yet the thing you have forgotten has simply hidden itself in some basement den. Suddenly it comes back to you with the utmost urgency. One would have to violently smash one's own skull, just like a computer hard drive, to be sure that everything one no longer wanted to deal with was finally erased.'

214 'No less problematic than adolescence is old age, a phase that has often been discussed of late, though no one can say when it begins. That can happen suddenly too—the French speak in such cases of a *coup de rieux*, and there is no shortage of stories about people who woke up one morning to find their hair snow-white.

'While Methuselah, according to the Bible, lived to the age of 969—a little more than Adam, who only managed 930—the lives of German men in Bismarck's day were usually over after a mere 36. But the median life expectancy, despite crises, climate change and environmental damage, increases by over two months annually in this country.

'In former times, great age seems to have been valued, perhaps even revered—people even spoke of wisdom. Now, however, the fear of Dr Alois Alzheimer's discovery from 1901 is the dominant feeling. This makes it ever harder to answer the simple question "How are you?"'

215 What constitutes a pest depends, at least according to Z., on one's perspective. The chemical industry, he says, has no doubts about its view on the matter. It considers the plant louse, the thrip, the sawfly and the spider mite creatures that can only be dealt with using their recommendable sprays. That also applies, as the package leaflets for their products state, to "other sucking and hidden pests". The respective researchers would never think of placing themselves in a corresponding category. From the perspective of the thrips, of course, it is humans that are the pests.

216 We love to rant about the newspapers. To many people, reading them is a sinful waste of time. 'That may well be,' said Z., 'but everyone should take a closer look at the printed matter they cannot stop reading. It would transpire that at least one German newspaper is among the best three in the world. Strangely enough, such a finding would be considered unseemly by the Germans, intimidated as they are by their own self-criticism. Yet this is suggested by the state of the English papers, which give the reader dirty fingers because their publishers even try to save on printer's ink. In the United States, the rule of the controllers has led to a gradual removal of foreign correspondents. But these costly people are precisely what is needed if one wishes to gain first-hand knowledge of the outside world.'

He would even go so far as to defend the arts section, a German speciality, against its lovers. One could spend many a leisurely hour wading through these bountifully blossoming lead deserts.

217 'One will often encounter magic spells there, presented in the form of reviews. One says that books, films, concerts and stage productions are *discussed* in the arts section, a procedure that is also common in the traditional treatment of warts. One can tell that the authors want to make every growth that bothers them shrink, or disappear entirely. Whether the witchcraft of discussion works, however, is unclear.'

218 On the topic of provocation, Z. said that it never got very far.

219 'I don't know if it's appropriate to return to the subject of money and its various states of matter. But perhaps,' said Z., 'you will allow me to recall a forgotten prophet who agonized over this in the past. Like many of his predecessors, he had an imposing full beard and was a vegetarian. His name was Silvio Gsell, and, naturally, his life was made a misery by being harassed by the authorities and mocked by those around him. Once, he reportedly served the Bavarian Council Republic as the people's commissioner for finance—an office that only existed for seven days, until the Reichswehr restored what it

thought of as order. The prophet was accused of high treason at the summary court martial, but acquitted because no one took him seriously.

'Conditions in Argentina, where Gsell opened a shop, gave him pause. This constant up and down between too much and too little, boom and crisis, deflation and inflation! He reached the conclusion that interest was to blame for this, and invented a simple way to put an end to the endless toing and froing. The solution to the problem was demurrage or scaleage, a currency that constantly lost value if one hoarded it rather than spending it quickly. "If there is a lack of money', said Gsell, 'a printing press is enough to multiply it, and if there is too much, one only needs an oven to burn it."

'Jeering from the economists of all schools and the politicians of all parties. Only a half-mad sectarian, they claimed, could have such far-fetched ideas. To this day, no one seems to have noticed that behind the backs of all Nobel laureates and Central Bank presidents, Gsell triumphed over his adversaries.'

Some of those gathered thought that Z. had once again gone too far with this claim and demanded that he retract it.

'Why? I see no reason to do so. The money in circulation today can quite rightly be termed demurrage. An object one could buy for a hundred dollars in 1945 costs 13 times as much today. I won't even get started on other currencies like the deichsmark, the forint, the Turkish pound or the peso. If you buy German government bonds with your money, you'll be punished with negative interest. Thus all debt, just as the prophet from St Vith in the Ardennes wished back then, vanishes into thin air. Because the amount of money increases immeasurably, billions have to be burnt—but an oven is no longer needed. Conversely, if some bank or other is lacking money, it need only report its need for funding and the printing press will immediately provide relief. One calls this procedure "quantitative easing". So, you see, there is no end in sight to the dance of St Vitus.'

220 'I see that many of you have brought umbrellas, even though there are no signs at the moment that there'll be any steady rain. That is wise, for one can never know what lies ahead. The need for protection has greatly increased of late, and, accordingly, umbrellas have become ever larger and more costly. Entire countries have slipped under them.

'That reminds me of a little adventure I had years ago in London. One fine June day, I was in the West End when a storm suddenly started brewing. Soon it was raining cats and dogs, as the English say. Luckily, on the corner of Piccadilly and St James's Street, I saw a well-stocked shop that sold walking sticks and umbrellas. Instructed by a helpful expert, I chose a robust black model with a solid handle. I was presented with a bill to the tune of £550. I was astonished. I didn't have this fantastic sum, so I had to cancel my purchase. I had stumbled into the most expensive shop in London.

'This episode occurs to me whenever I open a newspaper nowadays. For the bailout umbrellas currently being put up are even more costly than those in St James's, and so enormous that they can barely be folded up again. It is also unclear who will carry them— that is, under whose umbrella everything will be. The inventors of these contraptions insist that they are for rescue purposes; in that sense, it is natural to think of parachutes with which, if there are no alternatives left, one can jump out of a crashing aeroplane.

'I can only hope the umbrellas you've brought along are so cheap that one can always forget them and leave them standing around somewhere.'

221 'Have you ever considered what will happen if the crisis about which the media are constantly whispering troubling things in your ears does actually catch up with you? Naturally, I am only speaking of those who have a regular average income and pay their taxes and dues like good citizens, for this idea has long been familiar to everyone else. And I don't intend to bother you with stories about the time after the war, about returnees and refugees, which belong to you grandparents' repertoire.

'But what would it be like to make do with half of what you have? The advantage of such a consideration is that it opens up a back door for you—the only one that offers a way out of this chaotic economy.

'So, to make a few elementary suggestions: cancel your telephone service, terminate your insurances, rent out superfluous rooms, put away your car or motorbike and get rid of everything you don't need, assuming someone will buy it off you. No more mineral water, no restaurants, holidays only by tram as long as it's running. And aside from that: self-sufficiency, illicit work and the black market.'

'Maybe you're right,' countered the A-level student, sitting in the front row as usual. 'But such reflections remind me of hallway swimming. I hardly think they'll help us when the going gets tough.'

'Perhaps,' said Z. 'Nonetheless, it is better to be prepared for everything—even for the possibility that it won't even come to that. I fear I'm told old to worry in any case.'

222 On one of those tropical afternoons during an Indian summer, Mr Z. leant back on his bench, closed his eyes and mumbled that he was too tired to converse with us. Killing time was enough for him. Perhaps someone else could take the floor and, as far as possible, speak about something banal for a change.

'I find the bowler hat you always wear quite unbearable,' said the rather forward lady who, even in this weather, did not want to dispense with her tweed jacket and riding boots.

'The last place I saw something like that was in central London,' said someone else. 'But that's 10 years ago by now. On top of that, your hat's brown. A gentleman doesn't wear that sort of thing.'

'Beckett had a penchant for such headwear,' countered the A-level student, who was evidently well read.

'I've had this hat for a long time.' Z. stooped to explain. 'Back then I used to travel when I couldn't think of anything better. I found my bowler hat in La Paz. The Indio women have been wearing such things as long as anyone can remember, though nobody knows why. And you, do you know what's sitting on your head?'

The one he had addressed removed his purple baseball cap and held it out. On the front was an embroidered kangaroo with the letters 'AVK' underneath the logo. When asked, he had to admit that he didn't know what the inscription meant.

'Most people don't wear anything on their heads these days,' lamented the lady with the knitting things. 'What happened to the nice hats people had when we were young? The ones with the tea roses and veils? Now you only see them in the films.'

'My grandfather had an opera hat in his wardrobe,' related the discreet gentleman with the sunglasses, who had never spoken up before. 'And do you know what he taught me? An endless chanson of which I can only remember the first few lines:

A top hat is a lot of fun
if one happens to have one.

But a finer thing than that
is to have a second top hat.'

The conversation started to get out of control. Everyone had something to contribute. One man was annoyed by the monstrous helmets which the authorities wanted to force all cyclists to wear, the next wanted more turbans, the third supported the revival of the beret while the only art historian among them spoke out for the toque, the bagneuse and the sombrero but stopped short of the tricorn, the steel helmet and the burqa.

Z. blinked at the sun with satisfaction and contented himself with the remark: 'You see? Everything that's important can be left at that, especially in this heat.'

223 The autumn weather returned a few days later, and Z. immediately awoke from his sleepy frivolity and began his polemics again: 'The relationship between capital and work has been semantically ruined so thoroughly that anyone who has not lost their mind can only put their hands to their head. It starts with the linguistic somersault that the social partners perform by distinguishing between the employers who give work and the employees who take it. For it is the entrepreneur who takes the work, of course, and not vice versa. Otherwise he wouldn't pay for it.

'It's equally absurd when people speak of jobs. They are created, one says—an act that recalls Genesis. Then they must be maintained, saved, or, if it can't be helped, destroyed again. The most important difference between a place to work and a place to park is that the latter requires a fee to be paid while the former provides its owner with money. Time clocks and parking meters measure how much time has passed in each case.

'The question of what particular work is being discussed is never posed. Every job is worth honouring and is fiercely defended, even if it is a completely pointless, or even socially harmful, service.'

224 'I fear it will tire you if I list a few of them. Day after day, legions of tax accountants struggle with an impenetrable maze of regulations and directives; pitiable security personnel have to take away passengers' belts, perfume bottles and firelighters; dog units look for hashish stashes; curriculum researchers pester overtaxed teachers with ever new

reforms; corrupt sports functionaries spoil the expensive fun of some championship or other; and clueless advisors busy themselves with destroying intact companies. The elimination of these jobs and many others would be a blessing—one for which human society begs in vain.'

225 When an onlooker claimed to know that the lights in Europe would go out in 10 years at most, Z. pointed out that he would make himself unpopular with such prognoses. He had a right to do so, of course—see Cassandra. Nor should he fear, in this country, that he would be stabbed to death like Priam's daughter. But instead of saying 'I am right', he would advise him to exercise patience. In the best case, that is to say the worst, he could still say, 'I was right' or 'I told you so'. But Z. did not think much of the satisfaction this might offer the seer.

226 'I have an Italian friend,' Z. told us, 'who distrusts philosophers, especially those who turn an ordinary verb into a noun. They capitalize Being and decorate it with all manner of additions. They want to reprimand us with Being-thrown, Being-there and Being-in-the-world, to say nothing of Beyng with a *y* and the Being of Beings. He preferred to rely on the traditional inflection forms: I *am*, you *are*, he/she/it *is*, we *are*, you *are*, they *are*.

'He got by perfectly with those, and didn't risk ending up in some cloud-cuckoo-land.'

227 Towards evening, after Z. had said goodbye, someone made a disparaging remark about his secrecy—one really knew very little about him. 'Doesn't he have a family?' he asked. 'What does this man do all day? He doesn't seem to have a private life. What has Mr Z. got to hide?'

'Those questions are superfluous,' we responded to the troublemaker. 'We should be glad that he doesn't bother us with his life story, and that he keeps quiet about things that don't concern us.'

228 'Have it your way,' said the doubter. 'Ultimately, your Z. is just a braggart. I don't see why I should let him intimidate me.'—'But he likes it when people disagree with him.'—'So if he wants to share his thoughts, why doesn't he write a book?'—'Since when does a philosopher have to print what he thinks? We only know Heraclitus and Zeno through hearsay, just like Confucius and Jesus. And what was

Socrates if not a braggart?'—'No offence to Mr Z. but your analogies are flawed,' said a third man. 'To me, he seems more like a bored pensioner.'

229 Another time, Z. apologized for meddling in thermodynamics too—he was not a physicist, after all. 'But I know a few of the propositions they harp on about. Their first main theorem is that energy in a system can only be changed, not created or destroyed. The second theorem goes much further—it claims that entropy increases with every natural process.

'Wonderful! Except that there's one catch. For if one reads the small print, it says that all this only applies within a *closed* system. But is there even such a thing? Is the energy in what we call the universe constant? Is the world a closed system? I don't know, and I don't think the physicists know either.'

230 What is a hole? That was one of the equally naive and tricky questions Z. liked to come up with. Surfaces, he said, were rarely smooth—most formed lumps, hollows, tips and so on. But holes? Did a dent, a depression qualify? What about the skin and its pores? Did a hole not have to be permeable from both sides?

'Nonsense,' the boisterous A-level student called out from the front row, displaying the sole of his shoe. 'Would you deny that this shoe has a hole?'

'That's what I always thought too,' Z. replied, 'until a topologist explained to me that a hole is not a property of the surface but, rather, of the space surrounding it. If, for example, someone were at home on a lifesaver or a pretzel, it would never occur to them that their world had a hole in it. That, he said, was why mathematicians divide all objects into classes depending on how many holes they have. And they call this class the *genus*. I was baffled when I heard that. So a trouser button with three holes has a genus of three and a sphere zero. If, on the other hand, you view your own body as a tube— Lichtenberg reportedly suggested this—then, according to this logic, it would belong to the first of these classes.'

'Do you seriously believe that?'

'Granted, this perspective takes a bit of getting used to, but you can't deny its ingenuity.'

'And what use is it supposed to have?'

'Even though I know nothing about cosmology, I'd like to find out whether the universe is porous or has genuine holes. You only have to turn on the television and people are telling you about black holes. My topologist says that if the world had more than the normal four dimensions, we wouldn't even notice. He's used to dealing with between five and eleven dimensions, where one finds countless multiplicities and genera. Wormholes are evidently no rarity either.'

For his part, however—Mr Z. tried to reassure his listeners with these words—he was usually satisfied with those things that he could imagine.

231 A little heathenism couldn't hurt, Z. assured those who were still listening to him. Even the most unsuspecting person was, without realizing it, always surrounded by the ancient gods and goddesses. 'One doesn't have to study for that. One reaches for the remote control, and then the Olympiad is ringing in one's ears. The parcel delivery man wears the name Hermes on his shirt.* A glance at the calendar reveals that every weekday and month haunted by old idols, spirits and demons: on Thursday and Giovedí, Thor and Jupiter hurl their lightning bolts; on Friday and

* Hermes is the largest independent parcel service in Germany. [Trans.]

Venerdí, Freya and Aphrodite visit us; Sunday is ruled by Helios, Tuesday by Mars or Tyr, Wednesday by Woden and Saturday by Saturn.'

Z. concluded from this that it was not so easy to get rid of something pre-historical once and for all.

232 And that, he continued, did not apply only to our little continent, for all the planet's other inhabitants had grown accustomed to various things that had resulted from European ideas. There was a veritable chaos of time reckoning and calendars in the world, yet computers everywhere could only ever come up with the same year number, even if people had taken pains to replace additions like AD or BC with more neutral terms. Similarly, the metric units of the French, the scales of Celsius and Fahrenheit or the periodic table of Mr Mendeleev could be found everywhere.

It was difficult to say why all other continents had submitted to the achievements of the Europeans. 'All over the world one finds universities, railways, calls for democracy, logarithms, whisky bottles and spectacles. Those things may be blessings. But we should not forget that the machine gun, the concentration camp and terrorism are European inventions too.'

233 'Would you allow me,' asked Z., 'to say something about the art of refraining?'

That didn't go down well. An elderly gentleman in a wheelchair waved his hand dismissively after the first few words. But Z. wasn't so easily put off. 'Most people,' he lamented, 'simply can't stop, whether it's the expansion of an empire or a simple marital row. That's a pity.'

The chilly gentleman in the wheelchair was unwilling to accept that.

'Why?' he croaked. 'Most things stop by themselves if one waits long enough. Mother Nature sees to that by killing us one way or another. I don't see why we should come to her aid in doing so.'

'Dear friend,' Z. replied, 'it is laudable that you disapprove of suicide. But as long as some things do not stop of their own accord, we should prefer peace, even if we find it difficult.'

234 'I will assume,' said Z., 'that most of you own a computer. Then I daresay you know the many things such a device can remember, how quickly it can pore over entire encyclopedias and telephone books, and the absurd calculations with which it baffles us—despite getting smaller and smaller year by year. A wonderful toy!

'But have you ever wondered why these machines tend to rename everything? They call a love letter or a children's drawing a *document*. What we take to be a photo or a sonata is a *file* to them. Even though there is no desk in sight, let alone a surface, they would have us believe that we are dealing with a *desktop*.

'And that's just the beginning. Because a world opens up behind the *user interface* which is every bit as esoteric as that of the Hobbits. There are migrations without migrants and administrators whom no one ever appointed. Whoever ends up there will suddenly encounter a *registry* of which it is unclear what it registers, or magic places called *spool* and *shell*. Are they really shells or spools? There is also danger lurking in the BIOS, the *assembly* or in System 32. I can't possibly remember all that. I've written down a warning on a bit of paper. Here! It reads: AzSqlExt. dll and C_1142.Nls. Woe is me! Woe to the uninformed person who cannot boot! As soon as they press the wrong button, they will be carried off by the enigmatic but lethal Error 1321.'

'Yes, that's all a bit of a pain,' advised the cunning 17-year-old boy whose cap advertised the company syntec.com, 'but please don't smash your computer. It can't help it. The ones to blame for the whole abracadabra are its breeders, the engineers and programmers. They developed your hard- and software and instilled the machine with its barbaric sociolect. That's why you, the poor customer, now shrunken down to a *user*, would like nothing better than to throw the digital marvel against the wall and entrust yourself to the archaic media of pencil and paper.'

235 Another time, Z. quoted Osip Mandelstam, who supposedly said that attentiveness was one of the most important virtues for a poet. 'Unfortunately I know little about poetry,' said Z., 'but I think that his statement can be applied to all of us.'

236 On one occasion, Z. got onto the subject of the toilet. This facility, which had to endure such peculiar names as loo, bog or john, was the only place that offered a certain protection from the impositions of the outside world.

'It's not only a place where we can relieve ourselves in peace and quiet—it's also an ideal refuge for private reading. Nobody knows how many good ideas have come to people in this still place. And where else could they devote themselves to meditation without being disturbed?'

'But only until someone who's in a hurry bangs on the door,' countered the boy with the purple baseball cap who had suddenly reappeared but evidently had little time for the idyll Z. was describing.

237 'Recently, people have often been talking about reason of state again. What remains unclear is who can have this special form of reason. It presumably refers to persons who regularly meet at the so-called summits.'

'That reminds me of a forgotten Italian prime minister, who referred in 1914 to the *sacro egoismo* to which his government was entitled. But that is putting the cart before the horse, one is inclined to say—if anyone can summon a sacred egotism, it is at most the individual, assuming the reason of state leaves them no choice. Something of that kind happened in Berlin on 20 July 1944, to name only one example.'

238 'Nature's lack of regard for social justice is

evident in the fact that the ability to learn is unevenly distributed in every population. There are, at least, people everywhere who have no difficulties examining their ideas and increasing their knowledge. Some even do so with great pleasure. An experienced doctor needs only a few minutes to reach a diagnosis, a proficient cleaner will quickly find her bearings in a new household, and a prudent scientist must be capable of admitting a misstep in the laboratory. Without such abilities, a species like *Homo sapiens* would have died out long ago.

'Unfortunately, such gifts are only found on an individual scale. Collectives, on the other hand, are extremely reluctant to learn. The penny only drops when the pressure becomes so great that there is no other way out. As ever, a good way to understand that is to take a look outside one's front door. One world war was not enough to show the Germans that seeking world domination was not a brilliant idea. It took a second world war to convince them, and, even then, they waged that one to the last Volkssturm pipsqueak.'

That was, admittedly, a particularly strong example, Z. continued, but by no means an isolated incident. See Alexander, see Napoleon, see the Soviet

Communist Party, see a hundred other collectives that remained incorrigible until their downfall. And where the powers weren't great enough for complete self-destruction, gritting one's teeth and carrying on seemed to be one of the preferred approaches of every political class. To avoid admitting to its mistakes, it would cling to its obsessions until the disaster was complete.

239 'To paint yourself into a corner,' said Z. 'Do you know that one?' He had no idea how to say that in German. It had been a revelation for him when he heard the expression for the first time.

'So, you've been standing there for a few hours in your most worn-out clothes, the paintbrush in your hand and the paint pot next to you. And then you discover that you've made a mistake. Unfortunately, it's already too late. Before you lies a wonderfully smooth surface, shining and wet. You've painted yourself into the corner, and you can't get out of it without destroying your own work.'

'It's your own fault!' shouted the A-level student. 'Because you weren't careful.'

'So you think that sort of thing couldn't happen to you? Haven't you ever invested a great deal of time and effort in a project, a piece of work, an undertaking, and realized at some point that your sit uation will get worse with every step you take? So, to stay in the imagined picture, you'll take off your shoes and leave the room on tiptoe, even if you get fresh paint on your socks in the process.'

'That's not such a big deal!' interrupted someone who looked like a handyman. 'In a case like that, I'd just be glad if no one had seen me getting myself into such a mess.'

'So would I,' said Z. 'But things are less amusing if it is not an individual but a collective that has become trapped in a hopeless situation. For then one can't withdraw without paying a heavy price. Think of an army at war facing defeat, or of a polit- ical provocation. Whoever instigates something like that no longer cares about minimizing losses. They are more likely to carry on until everything is smashed to smithers, as a relevant marching song puts it. They think that by doing so, they can save what is most precious to them: prestige, which they mistake for their honour.'

He was glad, said Z., that things were usually more civil in this country. Even in the deepest peacetime, without any blood flowing, one could wreck the economies of entire countries as well as an amateurishly introduced currency. On a smaller scale, one could also study this approach in any provincial bank or pharmacy chain.

Carl von Clausewitz, that seminal strategic thinker, had already described this mechanism 200 years ago, and explained that retreat is the most difficult of all operations. Nobody seemed to have listened to him.

'It is a pity,' Z. concluded this reflection, 'that understanding is evidently only afforded to individuals, but never to human society!'

240 Z. had, once again, gone too far. 'I suppose you don't think much of democracy?' someone called out. A slender newcomer in the group highlighted the virtues of swarm intelligence but was rebuffed as a utopian and dreamer. The peaceful atmosphere among those present threatened to switch. 'Max Stirner,' another man interjected. '*The Individual and His Property*!'—'What property?'

Z.'s question was drowned out by the hubbub. A determined old lady who was attending for the first time swung her cane to underline her outrage.

'I don't have to listen to this,' she shouted. 'When you praise the understanding of the individual, I suppose you mean tyrants and people on killing sprees too? I know what I'm talking about because I'm very familiar with the Middle East!'

Z., who acknowledged all of this, fell silent for a while. Finally he conceded that he had indulged in exaggeration, and not for the first time. 'That's what comes of following a thought to its logical conclusion. This too is a mistake made more by the individual than the collective, and it leads directly to a dead end. This time I admit defeat.'

With that, peace was restored, albeit only temporarily.

241 The following day, Z. took his time holding forth about the pitfalls of similarity, as if nothing had happened. 'Show me a comparison that isn't flawed,' he challenged those present. When no one seemed willing to do so, he went a step further: 'Nothing incomparable exists. Whoever denies that entangles themselves in a logical contradiction. To issue a ban on comparisons, you see, you have to distinguish between the comparable and the incomparable, which means that you have already fallen prey to the

very thing you wish to ban.'

242 'You didn't let me have my say,' Z. complained.

'Why? When?'

'I mean the day before yesterday, when we were speaking about property. Things got so loud that one couldn't hear oneself speak.'

'What was on your mind?'

'That no one has managed to explain what we can really call our own. Is it one's own ideas? Does it refer to one's own DNA? A certain will of one's own? A goal? Does it turn out that it's about a home of one's own, or even one's own capital? It's all a complete mystery, but certainly in a class of its own.'

'True enough,' said the slender student. 'But that's not really what counts.'

And so, on that day at least, this question too remained open.

243 The cobbler profession was unfairly maligned, said Z. Instead of getting new soles for their boots, everyone relied on the countless shoe shops sprouting

up in the pedestrian zones of our cities. Repairs were replaced by the rubbish bin. He, however, found it somehow touching whenever he passed one of the few remaining invisible mending shops.

'After all, patchwork is still considered the non plus ultra in politics and economics. The ladies and gentlemen in charge spend their time patching ever-new holes. Budgets of billions, or trillions if those aren't enough, are used to stop the ladders that keep appearing in the fabric. New socks are evidently inconceivable.

'If the repairs fail completely, the time has come for surgery. Currency cuts must be carried out with a scalpel, metastases removed operationally and fractures mended. At the end, the patient is sewn up, but recovery, like peace, does not last forever. War destroys the freshly tiled roofs of homes again, and the helpers have barely left before it opens up new wounds. The fact that their help is only provisional makes them even more admirable.'

244 When someone challenged him to take a personal stance on the things he was talking about here, instead of—to continue the metaphor—patching

the work of those responsible, Z. quoted Alexander Herzen: 'Honesty and independence are my only idols. I wish to follow neither one flag nor another planted by this or that party.'

245 'You're not telling us anything new,' the pushy young philosopher called out. 'Are we doomed to rehash the same words over and over again?'

'Unfortunately,' said Z. 'That censorship is not a good idea, and that slavery is no fun for the slaves, is regrettably something that needs to be mentioned time and again, even if one has already heard it often enough. Politics is the eternal recurrence of the same. And not only politics! Culture is a ruminant too. Just take a look at the prefixes it comes up with: anything that starts with neo-, retro- or post- is old hat. One could almost believe that we can't think of anything new. So you see, I agree with you wholeheartedly, even if it doesn't suit you.'

246 'Are you afraid of hexameters? There used to be people who learned such verses by heart, even in Greek. But one doesn't necessarily have to do that. It's enough to swing with the dactyls— after five minutes you'll do it automatically, like learning to swim.'

Not everyone was convinced. One or two people who couldn't swim thought it wasn't so simple.

Z. said: 'If you like, I'll tell you how it was for
me. I only fly when I have no choice. At the airport,
one is bullied incessantly. On the plane, one constantly has some voice with unnecessary announce-
ments piped assaulting one's ears via loudspeakers.
But worst of all is when you have to spend an entire
night in one of these tin cans.

'Once, I had to travel to New York—please don't
ask me why. The flight takes around nine hours—
that's practically unbearable without an effective tran-
quillizer. Naturally, I had taken the necessary steps—I
had a handy a thin paper edition of the *Odyssey* in
my hand luggage. Being too uneducated to read
these 24 cantos in the original Greek, I'd obtained the
old translation by Johann Heinrich Voss.

'Instead of making me sleepy, the ron-ron-ron
of his hexameters kept me awake. The story is more
exciting than any thriller, and it's so catchy that one
can't put the book down.

'I turned down the tray of lukewarm chicken
and dispensed with opening the little bags, tins and
bottles I was offered. All I wanted was to be left in

peace. Shortly after Boston, as day broke, I read the last few lines:

> Son of Laertes and the gods of old,
> Odysseus, master of land ways and sea ways,
> command yourself. Call off this battle now,
> or Zeus who views the wide world
> > may be angry.
> He yielded to her, and his heart was glad.*
>
> The flight was over in no time.'

247 'Today I suggest we discuss the various forms of breath.

'I don't mean to offend the chemists, but I'm actually quite satisfied with the traditional four elements. I'd be perfectly happy with just fire, water, air and earth. I have no need of the few dozen trans-uranic elements that ambitious researchers have so far discovered or invented.

'You will raise the objection that air is not an ele-ment but a mixture of gases that we obtain, create, struggle for or gasp for, whether its nature is good

---

* Homer, *Odyssey* (Robert Fitzgerald trans.) (New York: Macmillan, 1998), p. 462.

or bad, thin or thick. How fantastically precisely this mixture is adapted to our lungs!'

'The reverse is the case,' countered our zoologist. 'We are the ones who adapted to the air. That's called evolution.

'Incidentally, most creatures do entirely without air. This element has only existed on earth for 350 million years. Whatever was here before that, for example a fair number of bacteria, have got by to this day with iron, sulphur, arsenic, nitrogen, methane and other substances. They simply breathe, if one can call it that, through their skin. They have no use for oxygen—it's almost poison to them.

'The rest of the earth's inhabitants had to grow accustomed to the new gas mixture in a laborious process. Animals like insects, spiders and fish had the idea of breathing through small openings or gills. That was a rather simple solution.'

'Now Mr Z. will no doubt bring up old Brehm again,' one of us mumbled.

But the zoologist continued his lesson unperturbed. 'Reptiles, amphibians, birds and mammals, on the other hand, just like us, insisted on developing a highly complex organ. To avoid having our breath taken away we need lungs, which means—tissues, penicillin, X-ray images, sanatoriums and so on.'

Z. had nothing to say again that. He silently lit a cigarillo. Several people in the group then started coughing, and a few others took off.

248 'I think it was an American woman philosopher who coined the phrase "historical luck". Sadly, I have forgotten her name. But you will understand immediately what she means. It doesn't take a horoscope for that—all one needs is some elementary knowledge of history and geography.

'Imagine you had been born as the daughter of a cook's maid in 1610, or as the son of a Jewish cobbler in Galicia 300 years later, or why not a few years ago as an orphan in Somalia. Extremely bad odds. Sooner or later you would most likely have starved to death or been murdered. Such a reflection deals a blow to the idea of justice from which it can barely recover, if at all.'

249 Z. was annoyed by the expression 'brain drain' which had established itself in the endless debates about migration.

'Millions of people leave their home countries because they hope to find something better than death elsewhere. These often include the best-trained inhabitants of the original country. Thus the talents of scientists, doctors, technicians and other professionals are beneficial to the society that takes them up while the region they have left moves deeper into poverty.

'Some people find such migration gains scandalous. But who are the objects of their accusations? Those fleeing their countries, or those who welcome them?'

To drain, Z. continued, meant to suck out or bleed dry. The country of immigration was thus presented as a neocolonial vampire that profited from the vitality of the fleeing.

'It is the other way around, dear self-accusers! For the truth is that we are dealing not with a brain drain but with a brain squeeze. Many, if not most, countries on the planet are ruled by people who do everything in their power to get rid of any native intellectual elements. Germany was also one of those countries a few decades ago, and we all know that, to this day, it has still not recovered from the expulsion of its greatest minds. A list of states that sabotage their own futures in this way would be a very long one.

'The consequences are barely foreseeable. While wrecked houses and mine-ridden streets, destroyed water pipers and clinics can be repaired within a few years, the talents that have been driven out cannot be replaced for generations. Warlords, dictators and kleptocrats leave behind not only scorched earth but also a hopeless vacuum in people's minds.'

250 'Even the most eager eulogist of biodiversity begins to stammer when the conversation turns to mosquitoes, bedbugs and ticks. That also applies to the human diversity of natural talents, one of which is stupidity. Its varieties are as numerous as those of lilies, just not as well-researched. Can I draw your attention to one of them that is usually underappreciated?'

One must distinguish, said Z., between comprehensive and partial stupidity. It was easy to spot a natural fool. It was a more awkward feeling when an intelligent person suddenly turned out to be an idiot. It was hard to know what to do in such situations. No brilliant scientist, no respected philosopher, no famous poet was immune to the danger of suddenly talking nonsense. One example was the German chancellor Angela Merkel, undoubtedly an intelligent woman, who had the audacity to make the idiotic statement 'If the euro fails, Europe fails'. Maybe, he thought, she would put her hands to her head as soon she came to her senses again.

What he meant by all that was simply that our intelligence was always treading on thin ice. An imperceptible stumble, and we would crash through it and sink into the floods of idiocy. The leisurely observer of such incidents was advised—if only in their own interests—to cover such slips of the brain with the mantle of distant brotherly love.

251 'The wish to make oneself invulnerable,' said Z., 'is one that humanity has entertained since time immemorial. The ancient Germanic peoples already sought to protect themselves with magic spells, roots, herbs and tattoos, and many African warriors still believe that some magic will make them bulletproof. One finds a diluted form of these tricks not only in any computer game but also among those who take part in public discussions.

'Some cite famous names or invoke supposed authorities, others think they can disarm any criticism by pre-empting it. What's even better is to pull the rug out from under one's opponent by having them guess the meaning of the respective oracular words. A further proof that we are dealing more with superstition than reason.'

252 'I must confess that I deceived both myself and you the other day. If one loses one's way in one's memory, it can make one believe all sorts of nonsense. I must apologize for that.

'It occurred to me too late that it was not a woman philosopher who had explained to the world what "historical luck" is. Evidently, I either dreamt up this phrase myself or confused it with another that comes not from an imaginary lady but from two renowned American gentlemen—namely, "moral luck". Now I remember: it was Thomas Nagel and Bernard Williams who introduced this concept. Here, the concern is no longer the sheer arbitrariness of birth but, rather, the question of accountability. A person is lucky in this sense if they have never been put to the test.

'What would you have done if... That's a question which invites contemplation. Only extremely conceited and self-righteous people will be willing to answer immediately in their own favour. So you can see that the problem is ill-suited as a party game. We should therefore turn our attention to a different subject.'

253 Z. pulled on one of his thin cigarillos and suddenly said that he sometimes thought of God. A few people groaned, but Z. was not to be stopped.

God was rather hard to find, he continued. In former times, one had known which way to turn—to Olympus, to Valhalla or simply Heaven. But now?

'Now, if we can believe theologians, one of God's attributes is omnipresence. But ubiquitous essentially means everywhere—not only in space but also in time and thus, if I have understood correctly, eternity.

'So it must be a sort of field, similar to the ether that was in fashion in the nineteenth century, when quantum physics was still in its infancy. Unfortunately we lack the organs, antennae and detectors to measure the spin, the charge of this phantom substance.

'Omnipresence is not always a blessing. Capital, the state and advertising strive for this status. One can only hope they will never quite attain it.'

But if the issue was a supreme being that was always and everywhere but never appeared, he did not see omnipresence as a threat. On the contrary— he, at any rate, found such a notion appealing. This time, Z. decided to leave it at that modest conclusion.

254 A sudden whirlwind swept through the tops of the old beech trees and tore the colourful leaves off their branches. 'We must make use of that. You know as well as I do that, among all those millions of leaves, no two are the same.'

'I can't believe that,' said one of the schoolboys who hung around there.

'You need only look closely, and you will see that I am right. A philosopher who died 300 ago taught me that. Shall we go?'

We hesitated, but the schoolboys enjoyed the game, picking the leaves up one by one and comparing them, while Z., standing up to his ankles in fallen leaves on a trail underneath the beech trees, was having fun rustling, rustling, rustling.

255 He often used to go to the cinema, or, far

worse, to the theatre, said Z. He got out of that habit. He preferred to have films, plays, television series and similar performances described to him instead. That saved a great deal of time. One didn't need to spend one's whole evening with it—it took 10 minutes at most to get an accurate impression. Anyone lucky enough to employ a cleaning lady should rely on her rather than some review or other. 'A fleeting acquaintance in a corner bar will also do the trick—to say nothing of you, who are so kind as to keep me company here.'

What was even more instructive than a single account was getting three or four different people to report what they had seen. It delighted him every time how inventive and confident these summaries turned out. Each person remembered only what they had found especially interesting, and cut out whatever seemed superfluous—which meant most things.

He had considered whether this procedure could also be applied to products of literary art, especially when the authors forced one to spend days or, indeed, weeks or months reading.

256 Z. wanted to know if any of us wished to expand our consciousness.

'I don't see why not,' replied his favourite adversary, the philosophy student.

'And how do you go about it?'

'There are all sorts of techniques to choose from. The mystics tested a few of them thoroughly. Or think of the Chinese and Indian traditions! Others prefer to experiment with drugs. But that's nothing new!'

'I see,' said Z. 'The question is simply what the point of it all is. Is it even desirable to keep inflating what we call consciousness ever further? Isn't there a danger that one's head will burst? Couldn't one take the opposite approach and gain relief by reducing one's consciousness? Throw out the accumulated baggage? Perhaps that would be more refreshing and healthy, even if there is little chance of achieving complete emptiness.'

'You're playing with words, as usual,' Z.'s opponent countered. 'That's exactly what techniques like meditation, yoga, Tao and so on aim for. Such training, which demands the utmost concentration, could just as easily be called expansion or renunciation. Those are just two poles of the same force.'

'Thank you,' said Z., 'for your explanation.' And

this time he even seemed to mean it.

257 'Temperate zone, my foot!' Z. complained. 'Soon this country will return to the time when one had to wrap up as soon as one left the house. Without a coat, scarf, gloves and sturdy shoes, existence will become a health hazard. And on top of that, it's getting darker by the day.'

He was right. The damp cold and the ground fog, which lingered obstinately over the meadows, had already put many of us in a bleak mood. Only the silent gentleman in the three-piece suit showed no signs of distemper.

As he later revealed to us, Z. had been on the verge of asking him if he would consider finally taking off his sunglasses. It occurred to him just in time that the silent guest might be blind. 'That's how easy it is,' he said, 'to overlook the most obvious things.'

258 Then two ladies with ponytails, wrapped in Norwegian-style pullovers, appeared, dragging a colourful mixture of animals on long leashes behind them.

'That's a veritable menagerie,' said Z.

'They're all just dogs,' said one man who knew

the park like the back of his hand. 'These two women look familiar. They're pros. It's their job to walk pets whose owners are too busy to spare 10 minutes so that they can get some fresh air.'

'Another one of these superfluous new professions with which superfluous people have to earn money,' Z. inveighed. 'How do you know they're dogs? One of them looks like a pouffe, the next like a calf, the third like a wig and the last one at the back is showing an arrogant demeanour like a foreshortened giraffe. Without a DNA sample, no one would ever think that these creatures belonged to one and the same species.'

'They're all breeding successes,' explained the dog expert. 'What you call a pouffe is a Pekinese, and you won't please any owners by confusing a Bolognese with a wig. It's not just that you have no idea—you simply don't like dogs!'

'The ugliest noise in all of nature is the constant barking of these beasts. They bite, they drool, they moult. And that smell! Naturally the so-called masters are to blame for all those grotesque deformities. One wouldn't want to encounter a wolf on a dark night, but at least it's not a tailor-made substitute for love.'

Z. would have done better to avoid broaching this subject, for he had now fallen out of favour with many of his listeners. 'I don't have to listen to any more of this,' called out an old lady who had previously always stood by Z. Others who had also followed him until that moment now turned away.

259 Turning to the few who were still holding out, Z. said: 'Winter is now upon us. In the time ahead, I will no longer be passing by here. I will find it hard to do without your company, whereas you, I hope, can dispense with me with a light heart.'

Some of us protested, but Z. dismissed all objections. 'I appreciate your courtesy,' he said, then picked up his hat and went on his way.

In Place of a Coda

We also left it at that. Just one, perhaps the last of the
faithful, couldn't find any peace after Z.'s farewell.
Though we advised against it, he made enquiries
which, as expected, proved fruitless. Neither the res-
ident registration office nor the passport authority
had ever heard of a man by the name of Zed.